CONTACT

WRAK-AYYA: THE AGE OF SHADOWS
BOOK FIVE

LEIGH ROBERTS

Editing by Joy Sephton http://www.justemagine.biz
Cover design by Cherie Fox http://www.cheriefox.com

Sexual activities or events in this book are intended for adults.

ISBN: 978-1-951528-06-5 (ebook)
ISBN: 978-1-951528-19-5 (paperback)

CONTENTS

Want a glossary of terms used in
Books One through Four?

Visit https://www.subscribepage.com/
eterachroniclesglossary1 to join my mailing list and
to get instructions on how to download the Glossary!

Dedication

To the Creator, who was the first to ever ask...

What If?

CHAPTER 1

K hon Tor, Tehya, Adia, and Acaraho stood on the platform at the front of the Great Chamber, hands clasped together and held high as they looked out at the smiling faces of the People. The Ashwea Awhidi had ended, and all were ready to move forward into the new chapters of their lives.

After the People quieted, the four stepped down from the front and wove their way into the welcoming crowd.

Adia was well aware that tonight would be the night she and Acaraho would consummate their pairing. Until now, there had been too much drama; one or the other, or both, had been too exhausted and neither wanted to spoil the experience. Though they had mated in the Dream World, this would be their first in waking time. Adia found her pulse racing in anticipation.

It was well past twilight by the time she and Acaraho arrived at her quarters. In spite of their low light vision, it was dark enough to create a warm, intimate atmosphere. The dried flowers and other decorations the females had put in place to celebrate their official joining were still there, though the fresh flowers had since wilted. The fluffy, over-stuffed sleeping mat—filled to unbelievable proportions to accommodate Acaraho's size and weight—was still waiting to be officially broken in.

Adia felt every beat of her heart in her pulse. *Why am I nervous? We have been together many times in the Dream World. Why would this be any different? But it is, it is!*

The rock slab door scraped along the ground as Acaraho easily pushed it shut. Adia jumped at the sound of it snapping into place. She looked around for something to pick up, fidget with, anything. Acaraho approached her, and with a finger under her chin, gently brought her head up so he could look into her eyes. He slipped his other hand around her waist and pulled her close. Her breath caught as she felt his hard body against hers. His kiss was soft and brief. He looked into her eyes again and then let his hand slip from her waist and intertwined his fingers in hers, leading her to the sleeping mat.

Adia was grateful that he was taking the lead. Why she should be nervous this time, she could not imagine.

Acaraho laid down and reached up for her, and she sat down next to him. He pulled her down into another kiss, this one longer and deeper. Her desire for him flared, and she slipped her legs down alongside the length of his and leaned over him while they continued to kiss.

"Finally, Saraste'," he said.

"I know, I thought this day would never come," she answered.

He brushed her hair away from her face, and running his fingers over her lips, he gently kissed her forehead. She lay next to him, and they stayed there a while, touching and exploring—in no hurry now for what they had so long only wished might one day be possible. Their kisses were becoming more impassioned, and Acaraho finally rolled her over, taking the advantage. Her insides clenched as he slipped his thighs between her legs, first one, then the other. His hands were under her hips, raising her to him, each movement making her longing for him flow quicker. She laid her palm along his face as they looked into each other's eyes. She placed soft kisses against his neck, the heat coming off him warming her and making her feel protected and safe. Her mind flashed back to the first moment she realized she cared for him, how it was an impossible situation as she could never be paired, yet now here she was, and the impossible was before her.

Adia ran her hands down his back to his hips and

pushed herself closer to him, signaling she wanted to wait no longer. Never breaking eye contact, Acaraho gently claimed her as his own. They found their rhythm with each other, relishing their first joining in waking time. At the moment of culmination, it seemed to Adia that *some last piece* had just fallen into place.

They held each other for some time before surrendering to sleep, savoring the changes in their lives that neither had ever dared hope would come to pass.

Back in the Leader's Quarters, Tehya and Khon'Tor sat in the eating area, Tehya stirring with her finger what remained of the Willow Bark tea that Nadiwani had brought her.

"What did you think of the assembly tonight?"

"I was nervous, standing at the front with you. I am not used to being the Leader's mate. I struggle with all the attention."

She continued to play with her tea.

Khon'Tor brought her free hand to his lips and pressed her fingers against them. Tehya smiled and lowered her gaze. He frowned playfully at the taste of her tea-stirring finger, making her laugh. He could not help but compare her to his first mate, Hakani. How two females could be so different, Khon'Tor did not know. He felt he had woken from a nightmare into a dream—a dream he did not deserve and one from which he was sure justice would one day force him to wake.

CHAPTER 2

Oh'Dar plopped onto his bed in the boarding house. The plain wooden frame with its hard mattress, the work table, lamp, and a stack of books on the bedside table comprised the sum of his existence at this point. He had no time or interest in anything else; he sponged up everything the teachers said. He only broke from studying to read his grandmother's letters. *What an amazing invention the Waschini writing is. What I'd give to be able to write a long letter to my mother and father at Kthama and let them know I'm alright.*

He lay back and tore open the latest missive from his grandmother. His eyes ran quickly over the pages, soaking up news about how life was going back at Shadow Ridge. He didn't mind that she wrote about the mundane; each word closed the distance between them. Oh'Dar's eyes drifted happily over the words from his Waschini home—until the last paragraph.

The letter fell from his hand and floated to the floor.

"*A large grey wolf has started showing up at Shadow Ridge.*"

There was no mention of what they were going to do about it, no mention of whether they'd already done something about it. Oh'Dar's stomach twisted. In his heart, he knew this was Kweeuu. Though it seemed impossible that the wolf could have traveled all the way from Kthama to his grandmother's, he couldn't shake the feeling that it was him.

Was it an omen to return to Kthama? Or was it just that the bond between them stretched so far that it had driven Kweeuu to take on such a dangerous journey? Or both? And why now, after so much time? And why there?

Oh'Dar would miss the last of his medical lessons at the hospital, but he didn't care. He shot around the room, throwing together the bare necessities to take with him. His schooling would have to wait; he couldn't bear it if they killed Kweeuu. On the off chance that a letter might get there before he would, he scribbled out a quick message and ran to post it.

It would be an unbearably long trip back to Shadow Ridge.

Kweeuu hung back in the woods as much as possible. He moved nervously in and out of the tree line, ears pricked at the unfamiliar noises. His nostrils flared at the pungent mixture of human and horse scents. He could find no fresh sign of his master.

Jenkins paced around the horse stalls, talking to each of the prize collection of the Shadow Ridge breeding line; mares, foals, and stallions. Dreamer pawed the ground and whinnied as Jenkins passed his stall. Dreamer was every bit the stallion they'd bred him to be, and the foals he threw were just as magnificent as their sire.

Jenkins picked up the rifle he kept leaned against his work desk, then set it back down. So far, something had kept him from killing the lone wolf. But if it went after any of the horses, there'd be no choice. Jenkins had taken to locking the horses up at night, hoping the animal would go away. However, as the heat of the summer deepened, he couldn't continue to do so.

Oh'Dar endured the long stagecoach journey back to Shadow Ridge. If he'd had Dreamer with him, he could have made it in a third of the time. The further they traveled, the more uncomfortable every bump and jostle made him. Since it was virtually impossible to sleep, he had lots of time to think.

So much had happened since he'd left Kthama and his adoptive parents to find whatever might be left of his White family. He knew that his mother, Adia, would find the message he'd left. He was sure that between her and his father, Acaraho, they'd have figured it out.

"I have left to find the Waschini. Please do not try to find me. Please let me go."

But what it couldn't convey was the anguish and heartache that had led up to his leaving.

Did they think he'd left casually? And right after Acaraho, with some of the guards and females, had worked so hard to set up his workshop so he would have a place of his own. He knew they were aware that he struggled with fitting in. As a Waschini child raised by the People, he'd learned everything he could about being one of them, but none of it had changed the fact that he was *not*. His struggle to find his place had been brought to a head when Oh'Dar overheard the Leader, Khon'Tor, telling one of the watchers that it was just a matter of time before Oh'Dar would bring disaster to the People. And Khon'Tor had said that when it did, the blame would fall on Adia's head for bringing him there.

It now seemed so long ago. Oh'Dar had planned well, gathering the supplies he needed for the long trip, including carriers with the water-tight pattern that, with his greater dexterity, only he among the

People was capable of weaving. He'd fashioned clothing that didn't look like any of the Brothers' designs. He'd waited over the months, building up the courage to set out on his own. It had broken his heart to leave them, but he couldn't live with the fact that he might cause harm to his mother and to the People—or worse. And now, after all this time, had Kweeuu truly found his way to Shadow Ridge? Oh'Dar shuddered to think of the perils of that journey.

When Oh'Dar had left Kthama, Kweeuu was a young and lanky adult not yet having reached his full bulk. By now, he'd be full-grown, and any Waschini seeing the wolf would very likely kill him. Oh'Dar prayed to the Great Mother that he would make it back in time.

Oh'Dar's grandmother, Mrs. Morgan, sat with her morning tea as the housekeeper brought Oh'Dar's letter. Once Mrs. Thomas had left, Mrs. Morgan opened it carefully and took out a single sheet of paper. She read the scribbled lines, then set down her teacup and swept off to the stables to find Mr. Jenkins.

Mr. Jenkins had just finished grooming Dreamer and was giving a final last stroke down the stallion's gleaming coat when she came running up, out of breath.

"Ben!" she called to him, the piece of paper clutched in her hand.

Mr. Jenkins put down the brush. "What is it, Vivian?"

"Grayson is on his way back. I just got this today. Look."

He unwadded the letter which had suffered in her hurried journey from the house, and quickly read the few words scribbled on an otherwise blank page. *"On my way back. Do NOT kill the wolf, I beg of you—Grayson."*

"Do NOT kill the wolf, I beg of you." He must have been in a terrible hurry to write only that—or he needed you to know how important it was. When was this posted?"

"Long enough ago that he should be here any time now," said Mrs. Morgan. Tension crossed her face as the flurry of things to take care of ran through her mind—her grandson was coming home!

"How does he know about the wolf?"

"I must have told him about it in my last letter. I don't remember writing much other than it had shown up and has stayed around." She was distracted now, her heart happy at the thought of his return.

"Well, I'm glad I haven't shot it yet. But this is a mystery. I don't know if we'll ever be told where Grayson has been all these years, but if he ever decides to confide in us, I'm sure it'll be a story for the ages."

Mrs. Morgan knew Mr. Jenkins well enough to realize how worried he was with the wolf around the horses. It could easily scare them until they ran themselves to death.

Mr. Jenkins put his arm around her waist and walked her back to the big white house; there was much to do to get ready for Grayson's return.

By Mrs. Morgan's calculation, Grayson's lessons weren't quite over. The young man was coming all this way, interrupting his medical instruction over a wolf. *And just what is he going to do about it when he gets here?* she thought. *My grandson is a mystery, to be sure.*

Oh'Dar was almost at Shadow Ridge. As much as he wanted to see his grandmother and the others, oh, how he prayed they hadn't killed Kweeuu. He didn't know if he could bear that. And if it was an omen for him to return to Kthama, how was he going to break that to his grandmother? It was one thing for him to go away, preparing for his future. It would be another thing for him to leave and return to his past.

When the stagecoach reached the town nearest to Shadow Ridge, not wanting to waste time waiting for someone to fetch him, Oh'Dar was obliged to hire a carriage for the last stretch.

It was early evening when he reached the ranch.

He saw Jenkins coming out of the barn as the horse and carriage pulled up.

Dusty and exhausted, Oh'Dar was longing for one of Mrs. Thomas' warm baths, but it would have to wait. First, he had to find out if Kweeuu was still around—still alive.

"Grayson!" Mr. Jenkins came running to meet him. He hugged the young man and put an arm around his shoulders.

"Let's get you up to the house; your grandmother has been beside herself waiting for you."

"Did my letter make it here?"

"Yes, she received it. A wolf, son? Did you come all the way back here over a wolf? We cannot wait to hear about this."

"Is he still here?" Oh'Dar held his breath as he waited for the answer, his eyes scanning the horizon.

"Yes, he's still here. Biggest darn animal I've ever seen. Hangs out on the ridge, way back in the tree-line. So far, he's not bothered anything, just paces back and forth when he's not simply sitting there," explained the stable master.

Oh'Dar breathed a deep sigh of relief, and they headed together to the big house.

The two men walked up the long flight of front stairs, and as they came in through the front entrance, Mrs. Thomas appeared, as she always did, as if by magic.

"Master Grayson!" Even she couldn't help but embrace the young man. "Your grandmother is in the parlor; come on, she's done nothing else but watch for your arrival. Thank goodness you're here; perhaps now she can get some rest."

Mrs. Morgan was seated on the large floral sofa. Oh'Dar had forgotten how many patterns there were in all the rooms. It was one of the first things that had struck him—along with the fact that all the Waschini structures were straight lines and hard angles, little like what was found in nature. A large part of what the People believed about the Waschini was true— they didn't seem to live in concert with the Great Spirit. It was as if they'd lost their way somehow and were drifting along, unable to connect back. He believed it to be the Waschini's greatest source of unhappiness. To be lost and know it was one thing; to be lost and not know it was a nearly hopeless situation.

"Grayson!"

Oh'Dar hurried to his grandmother and embraced her before she could even rise. He breathed deep. She smelled of lavender and roses, and it always reminded him of the scents in the quarters of his adoptive mother, Adia. But Mrs. Morgan was much softer and rounder than any of the People, which made her eminently huggable.

"I'm so glad you're here. We've missed you so. Everyone has. Are you tired? Do you need to rest? Your letter caught us all off-guard. A wolf, Grayson? Please tell us what this is about."

She was losing the battle to hold back her tears of joy.

"I am tired, Grandmother. It was a long, uncomfortable ride."

"It is so good to have you back home, but you're early. Did your studies end early? When do you have to be back at the hospital?"

"I left the moment I got your letter. As to when I go back, it depends on what happens with Kwee—" he stopped himself. "The grey wolf."

Oh'Dar looked down, shifting uncomfortably beside his grandmother. He knew they were curious to know about his past. But he'd never revealed any of it, for fear of bringing Khon'Tor's prediction to pass—that he'd be the reason for the fall of Wrak-Ayya, the Age of Shadows that the Ancients had predicted would threaten the People's entire way of life.

Oh'Dar had lived among the Waschini for over two years now. Other than Louis, the uncle who'd arranged for the murder of him and his Waschini father and mother, Oh'Dar had seen none of the ruthlessness and barbarity that the People's stories told about the Waschini. On the contrary, from the moment he'd walked into the Waschini settlement and Mrs. Webb and Grace had taken him into their care, and also throughout his time at Shadow Ridge, he'd been met only with warmth and hospitality.

Whatever they imagined his past to be, Oh'Dar assumed it involved the Brothers. They couldn't possibly imagine the truth. He wondered if they could be trusted with knowing the existence of the People. If any Waschini could, it would be his grandmother and Mr. Jenkins.

Mrs. Morgan interrupted his thoughts. "Do you want to go upstairs and rest before dinner, Grayson? What would make you feel better after that long ride?" They'd worked hard to get his room ready for him with fresh linen, and all his clothes re-washed, dried, and ironed.

Oh'Dar thought for a moment and then turned to the housekeeper.

"Mrs. Thomas, would it be possible to have one of those wonderful baths that you draw?

"Certainly, Master Grayson. I'll come and get you when it is ready." She smiled and went off to prepare a steaming tub for the young man.

Lost in his thoughts, Oh'Dar let out a huge sigh. He knew what he had to do now, but how to tell his grandmother? He decided to leave that for a while; she was so happy he was home that he didn't want to spoil things by telling her he'd be leaving in a few days. And not to return to school but to return to somewhere he could never tell her about and which she couldn't imagine in her wildest dreams.

Before long, Mrs. Thomas came to fetch Oh'Dar.

As he eased himself into the soothing, warm water and relaxed, he thought through the supplies he'd need for the journey home. He'd need some Waschini clothes for the start of his travels, and if they still fit, the clothes in which he'd arrived—to change into later. He'd need water bottles, dried fruits, and nuts, as well as anything else that would keep for the long trip. It was a lot to put together; it might take him longer to prepare than he'd thought. He wished he had a weapon, but there was no time to make a bow and arrows. He could fashion a spear such as the Brothers and the People used but decided it was not a weapon a Waschini would be carrying. He would have to ask his grandmother for one of her horses. As much as he'd have loved to take Dreamer, Oh'Dar knew he couldn't because the stallion was too valuable. But oh, how he loved riding that horse, and with Dreamer, they'd make better time getting back than it had taken him when he first sought out the Waschini on foot.

Oh'Dar couldn't help but let his thoughts wander to Adia and Acaraho—the only mother and father he'd ever known. *How will they be doing? What will have happened since I left? And what about Nootau? By now, Nootau will tower over me even more than before. The last I saw my brother, he had all the promise of inheriting our father's massive build.*

Kweeuu cannot stay here; I have to take him back to safety. But what about Khon'Tor's declaration that I'll bring disaster to the People. Am I to be the cause of some catastrophe? Is it safer for the People that I stay away?

In a fight between the People and the Waschini, without their man-made weapons the Waschini wouldn't stand a chance. But Oh'Dar knew what the

Waschini weapons could do. Jenkins had taught him how to shoot both a rifle and a pistol. He had nothing but fear and respect for the White Man's guns.

The water cooled, and Oh'Dar stepped out of the tub. He put on the clean clothing Mrs. Thomas had laid out for him. Morning would come soon enough, and that meant one day closer to telling his grandmother he'd be leaving all too soon.

As the first rays of morning broke through his window, Oh'Dar was already pulling on his boots. The smell of breakfast cooking tempted him sorely, but it would have to wait, and he practically flew down the stairs.

Mrs. Thomas and Miss Vivian appeared just as he ran outside. The housekeeper threw down her kitchen towel, and not wanting to miss the excitement, both women hurried after him.

Once outside, Oh'Dar scanned the ridge for any sign of the grey wolf. Seeing nothing, he crossed into the paddock and started walking across the pasture toward the rise. Within moments, Mr. Jenkins was running after him, rifle in hand.

Oh'Dar heard the stable master following, and he stopped short at seeing the weapon. "What is *that* for?"

"Just a precaution, Master Grayson. I cannot take

a chance of you being mauled to death, and especially not in front of your grandmother."

With that remark, Oh'Dar saw both his grandmother and Mrs. Thomas pressed against the fence, watching everything.

Oh'Dar raised his palm toward Mr. Jenkins.

"You have to trust me, please. Please, you cannot harm him. I won't take any unnecessary chances."

Oh'Dar tramped across the field toward the ridge.

Seeing no sign of the wolf, he cupped his hands around his mouth and called out in his native language, "Kweeuu, come!" He'd never taught Whitespeak to Kweeuu.

As Oh'Dar called, Mr. Jenkins turned to look back at Mrs. Morgan and shook his head at the foreign sound.

With no sign of the wolf, Oh'Dar kept walking. He was now nearly at the crest of the rise. Finally, he spied movement in the shadows.

Oh'Dar crouched down as he'd done when Kweeuu was young, and which had always brought the cub clambering to him.

More movement.

Finally, a large furred head broke into the light. It was him. It was Kweeuu. Oh'Dar almost cried, glad his back was to the others.

Kweeuu broke from cover. Racing toward Oh'Dar in great leaps, the giant grey wolf covered the distance in seconds. The young man reached out his arms just as Jenkins took aim.

Kweeuu landed on Oh'Dar with a resounding thud, bowling them both to the ground. To those who didn't know better, it looked like Grayson was being mauled to death.

From the fence, Mrs. Morgan called out, *"Ben!"*

Mr. Jenkins took aim, his finger on the trigger, but was unable to get a shot with them tumbling together. Then, instead of screaming, they heard laughter coming from the rolling bundle of young man and fur.

Both women stood transfixed, their hands over their mouths as Oh'Dar and the giant wolf played together, the wolf jumping away and then back again in abject glee at having found the young man. Jenkins lowered his rifle.

By now, Oh'Dar was covered in leaves, grass, dust, and wolf slobber. He was laughing joyously.

Once he'd calmed down, Oh'Dar rose to see if Kweeuu would follow him over to the others. Kweeuu took a few tentative steps, but that was it.

Wanting to reassure his grandmother and the others, and curious as to whether the wolf would remember, Oh'Dar gave Kweeuu a few commands.

"Sit," and the wolf sat.

"Lie down," and the wolf lay down.

Finally, "Roll over," and after a moment's hesitation, Kweeuu rolled over, paws akimbo.

Oh'Dar knew he was showing off a bit, but he wanted them to see Kweeuu more as a pet than the giant predator they thought him to be.

Finally, the young man gave Kweeuu a sign to let him know he could return to his comfort zone and then turned to join the others. He looked back to watch the wolf cross the pasture and disappear again into the cover of the wood line.

Oh'Dar dusted himself off as he approached Mr. Jenkins and the two women. He was amused by the look on all their faces.

"Damndest thing I ever saw, Master Grayson." Mr. Jenkins was the first to speak.

"Mrs. Thomas, do you have anything I could feed Kweeuu?"

Oh'Dar hated to ask, but he didn't want the wolf out hunting so soon before taking him back to the safety of Kthama.

"I'm sure I can find something."

"Won't that just keep him around?" Mrs. Morgan's voice faltered a bit.

"Yes, that's the point. I don't want him wandering off Shadow Ridge to hunt; it would just put him at risk. As it is, I cannot believe he found me—and that he made it here safely."

Over the next few days, Oh'Dar kept Kweeuu fed and prepared himself mentally for their journey. Finally, he could stall no longer; he had to tell them he'd be leaving in a few days with no idea when he'd return.

His chest tightened as he looked for them.

"Grandmother, Mr. Jenkins, there is something I have to tell you. I know it isn't what you want to hear, but it is something I have to do. I'm sure you still have your first questions about my past, and now I've just added a hundred more. I hope that someday I'll be able to tell you everything. But for now, I cannot."

Mrs. Morgan pressed her hand against her chest as if her heart was about to break.

"I'm so grateful, Jenkins, that you didn't kill Kweeuu. As you saw, we have a past relationship."

Despite the seriousness of his tone, Mr. Jenkins had to smile at the choice of words.

"Kweeuu came here to find me. But he cannot stay here. And it means that for his own safety, I have to take him back."

Mrs. Morgan found her voice. "Back? Back to where? You mean back to wherever you were all these years, Grayson?"

"Yes. I have to take him back to where he'll be safe and somehow make him understand that he has to stay."

"How long will you be gone? What about your schooling?"

"It's a long journey, Grandmother. All I can say is I will come back as soon as I can. And *I will come back*. As for my schooling, that decision will have to wait until I return." Oh'Dar looked directly at her, holding her gaze with his striking blue eyes.

Mrs. Morgan laid down the fork she'd been holding and put her hands in her lap. Oh'Dar knew the last thing she wanted was for her grandson, missing all these years, to return to wherever he'd been—with a grey wolf in tow—not knowing when he'd return.

She looked across at Mr. Jenkins, tears rimming her eyes. He reached over and took her hand.

Oh'Dar smiled very briefly to see the affection pass openly between them. He hated to leave his grandmother again, but it was comforting to know that they were finally admitting their feelings for each other.

"What do you need for this journey, son?" Mr. Jenkins asked.

"We'll be covering a great distance. It would help if I could borrow a horse. I know it is a lot to ask. But if there is one I could use, it would cut a great deal of time off the trip. And I could start getting him used to Kweeuu now. Sometimes horses think of wolves as more like dogs—so it may not be a problem, but I have to see. And I'll need supplies for the trip. Nuts, dried berries. Beef jerky if we have it." Then almost to himself, he said out loud, "I wish I had a bow and a quiver of arrows."

Every word he spoke was a clue that he knew they were soaking up.

"How soon do you want to leave?" asked Mr. Jenkins, adding, "You'll need several saddlebags to hold everything."

"As soon as I have everything ready," answered Oh'Dar as tears spilled from his grandmother's eyes.

Though it would be easier to wait and travel in the cooler Autumn weather, he needed the deciduous trees and bushes to provide cover, and it would be dangerous to keep Kweeuu near Shadow Ridge for that long.

He sat down next to his grandmother, and leaning over, hugged her hard.

The days passed too quickly, and before long, they were ready to leave. Mr. Jenkins had picked Storm for Oh'Dar to ride because when not riding Dreamer, Storm was the young man's second choice, obeying his commands without question. Jenkins knew Storm would carry Oh'Dar safely to his destination, wherever that was.

Everyone had contributed generously to his trip. Multiple saddlebags were packed with dried foods, nuts, and the jerky. Oh'Dar had packed his original traveling clothes, the ones he'd made at Kthama, designed not to resemble the Brothers' clothing. They no longer fit very well, and he'd have to alter them once he got home to his workshop. Unfortunately, he'd have to travel the entire distance in Waschini clothing. He had his original water bottles but chose instead to use the canteens Mr. Jenkins had provided. Oh'Dar studied the drawing that the stable master had prepared, and that showed the way back to where Mrs. Webb and Grace had found him.

Once there, he'd have no trouble finding his way back to Kthama. The trick was to do it as circuitously and stealthily as possible.

They stood in a circle on the dirt driveway, saying their goodbyes. Multiple embraces and many tears later, Oh'Dar threw his leg up over the saddle, the leather creaking under his weight. Mrs. Morgan looked up at her handsome grandson. He was no longer the adolescent who'd come to them almost two years ago. He was now a man, and she wondered how old he'd be when she saw him again.

Oh'Dar's chest was tight, and he couldn't bear to stay in that place of heartache any longer. He turned Storm to leave and called out to Kweeuu. The grey wolf appeared out of the woodlot and started padding after them. At the end of the drive, Oh'Dar turned to check that Kweeuu had indeed caught up. So far so good, Storm seemed not to care that the giant grey wolf was loping along with them.

They covered as much distance as they could during twilight and dusk, but avoiding daylight travel had extended the trip. Oh'Dar supplemented his supplies with whatever he could find along the way. After the third week, he could no longer stand the dried cran-berries, raisins, and nuts. He dismounted and looked into the larger saddlebag that he had not yet opened.

His fingers brushed hard steel. He jerked his

hand out as if he had touched a Sarius snake. He knew exactly what it was. It was the same pistol that Mr. Jenkins had used to teach him how to shoot. After Oh'Dar's uncle had pulled a gun on him in the stables, Mr. Jenkins had taught Oh'Dar how to use a rifle and a pistol.

Oh, Jenkins, I know you meant well. And I could certainly use some fresh game at this point. But what I'd trade right now for a nice quiet bow and quiver of arrows.

Oh'Dar laid down the map Jenkins had made him. If this was correct, he should be close to the town where Mrs. Webb and Grace had befriended him. He could not stop there with Kweeuu in tow but wished he could see them again.

He circumvented the town and finally found familiar ground—the trail he had covered on foot from Kthama. *Oh, how I wish I could navigate using the magnetic lines, as the People do. But at least I could learn how to use the stars.*

Oh'Dar made another mark on the Keeping Stone he had brought for this trip. At least he would know how long the return trip would take him. *Whenever that will be.*

Once he was a safe distance past the town, he camped out for a couple of nights, giving Storm a rest and Kweeuu time to hunt. He looked up at the canopy of stars and dreamed of home—at least the first home he had ever known.

One of the watchers shifted his position on the thick branch, thinking he spotted movement in the tree line on the far high ridge. He cupped his hand over his eyes to cut the sun's glare. Squinting, he could make out two figures, one which looked like someone on horseback and another trailing behind. It could not be what he thought.

They were still a way out, but he raised his head to the breeze and caught their scents. The watcher made his way carefully down from the treetop to notify the Brothers that a Waschini on horseback was indeed headed toward their territory, accompanied by a wolf.

Chief Ogima nodded as he received the news. They had become accustomed to the Waschini traveling through. It was an uncommon occurrence, never amounting to the threat the High Council had warned about years ago. Is'Taqa thanked the watcher and said they would station some braves along their perimeter, relieving the Sasquatch watchers just in case. It was one thing for the Waschini to see the

Brothers; it would be a catastrophe for them to come across any of the People.

The warm 'second summer' was in full force. Warm breezes promised cooler ones to come. Oh'Dar was getting close to the Brothers' village, and he wondered if anyone would recognize him riding in on the big, grey stallion.

Pounding hooves sounded up over the rise before Oh'Dar as four braves on painted ponies rode up to intercept him. Storm startled, but Oh'Dar brought him under control. He gave Kweeuu the sign, "Leave," and pulled up between the wolf and the braves.

"Greetings," Oh'Dar said, in the language of the Brothers and the People.

The braves looked at each other cautiously, clearly confused at a Waschini talking to them in their own language.

They do not immediately recognize me on this horse, with my hair cut, and in these clothes.

"It is me, Oh'Dar, son of the High Protector of the People, Acaraho, and their Healer, Adia." Oh'Dar pulled off the black hat he sported so they could see his face more clearly.

One of the last braves to arrive pulled his pony forward. He stared for a moment and then exclaimed, "Oh'Dar!"

"Pajackok!" Oh'Dar was relieved to see his long-time friend, and they greeted each other exuberantly.

"I am on my way home to Kthama. I want to stop and rest on the way and visit with Second Chief Is'Taqa and Honovi, and with Chief Ogima Adoeete if he has time."

Pajackok and the other braves turned around to lead him to the village. As they left, Oh'Dar called to Kweeuu, and the grey wolf came bounding after him. The braves smiled to see the large animal racing toward them.

Oh'Dar enjoyed their natural acceptance of Kweeuu—he would not have gotten that reception in a Waschini village.

As the riding party came over the hill, all heads in the village turned their way. The braves skidded to a halt as Oh'Dar rode up between them and pulled Storm to a stop.

Is'Taqa and Honovi came out of their shelter with two others in tow. They both stood for a moment, squinting at Oh'Dar before recognizing him. A girl and a young woman stood behind them, peeking around to see who it was.

"Adik'Tar Is'Taqa. It is me, Oh'Dar! And Kweeuu!" he called out to them.

The couple came running over to him as he dismounted, and together they clasped him in a warm embrace. Then Honovi pushed him back and held him at arm's length. She fingered his short, dark black hair, then examined his traveling wrappings, which were very dusty from the trail.

"I do not remember you being so tall," she remarked.

"A lot changes in a short time. But I think it is partly the boots," and he lifted a foot to show her.

"Are they as uncomfortable as they look?"

"Unbelievably so," and they laughed.

"Please, Honovi, how are my parents?" He was afraid to ask because he had stayed so long.

"They are both fine. Oh, they will be so happy to know you are back!"

"May I stay a night before going home? I hate to take another day to return, but I am very tired, and both Storm and Kweeuu need rest."

"Oh, of course. We can sit by the fire as we used to. Some of the braves will take care of your horse." She turned to the others who were still watching, and Pajackok nodded.

Then she pulled Acise forward.

Oh'Dar caught his breath at the beautiful young woman standing in front of him.

Acise smiled at Oh'Dar and then looked away. Finally, Snana came running over, buckskin skirts flying, and asked if she could pet the wolf. Oh'Dar gave Kweeuu the command to sit, and he sat—to everyone's entertainment. He re-introduced Snana to Kweeuu, who tried his best to lick her to death.

"I have some fresh wraps for you if you would like to bathe. I know how much you loved swimming in the pond. I think it is still warm enough. Then you could warm yourself by the fire. I will get some food for Kweeuu," said Honovi.

Oh'Dar had forgotten how much he loved the water. He nodded, and Honovi went to get him what he would need for his swim.

Oh'Dar eased himself into the clear, refreshing water and breathed a sigh of relief. He had not realized how much stress he was under. He floated for a while, enjoying the familiar sights and sounds. He let his thoughts return to the many times before when he had done just as he was doing now. The People did not particularly care for the water, but he could never get enough of it, and he had missed the silky coolness flowing over his skin, the carefree sense of buoyancy in such a large body of water. All the stress of the journey drained from him just as did the dust, and for the first time in a long time, he truly relaxed.

He would have enjoyed a longer soak, but having been away longer than he felt comfortable, he decided to get back. He swam over to the edge and hoisted himself out onto the soft loam. Just as he got to his feet, he heard a rustling in the bushes. It did not take him long to spot his visitor. He pretended not to see Acise peering at him from the dappled undergrowth.

Oh'Dar dressed and returned to the village,

letting Acise think she had gotten away with spying on him. He decided he would tease her about it later when he got to know her again.

After enjoying a meal with real substance to it, and after tossing Kweeuu the scraps, Oh'Dar sat at the fire with his second family, as they had done many nights before. The warmth from the licking flames was soothing. The smell of burning wood around the village fire knitted his two lives together for just a moment, reminding him of his times around the farmhands' evening fires with Jenkins at Shadow Ridge.

He could not help but notice Acise and tried to see, in the graceful woman sitting here now, the little girl he used to tease and play with. He caught her staring at him several times in return. *Have I changed as much as she has in this short time I have been away?*

Seeing he was falling asleep sitting up, Honovi spoke up, "Oh'Dar, please. We know you are exhausted, and our curiosity can wait until you are ready to talk about it."

The family chat was comforting, and Oh'Dar appreciated that they did not pelt him with questions. He knew his friends must be anxious to know where he had ended up and what he had been doing, but out of respect for his exhaustion, they just spoke lightly about mindless topics, letting him take the lead in guiding the conversation.

"Thank you, Honovi. It has been a long journey, and I am so tired. But I will tell you that I set out to find my Waschini family, and I did indeed locate them. I was with them almost the whole time I was gone. I have been studying their medicine, their Healer ways. I am anxious to share the differences in their approach with you and Ithua. They live quite differently from how we do. There's so much to tell you," he sighed.

"We understand. Please go to bed whenever you want. I have made up a place for you in our shelter, as before. We will all be in later."

Oh'Dar thanked her and nodded to each of them. Then he excused himself and went to their shelter to turn in. Kweeuu followed the young man inside and lay down next to him, the warmth of the furry body pressed against his back now a familiar comfort. It was the soundest Oh'Dar had slept since he left Shadow Ridge.

Word spread quickly to Kthama that Oh'Dar had entered the Brothers' village. Acaraho stood with the watcher who had brought the report, listening carefully to his descriptions. Other than the grey stallion and Waschini clothing, everything else fit, including the grey wolf. It would also explain Kweeuu's being gone so long.

After all this time, Oh'Dar had come home!

Acaraho wanted to find out whether it was Oh'Dar before he got Adia's hopes up. She had never stopped believing he would come back to them someday.

Rested, Oh'Dar spent the following day telling Is'Taqa, Honovi, and Ithua about his experiences, and answering questions about the Waschini ways while Acise listened to every word with rapt attention. The day seemed to fly by.

"I am sure you are anxious to get to Kthama," said Is'Taqa later.

"Yes. I will leave at first light tomorrow morning. Storm has had enough rest by now, and I am sure that word of my return has already reached Kthama."

As Oh'Dar was finishing his sentence, they all heard the commotion. A crowd had gathered toward the edge of the village as a large figure came down and out of the brush.

Oh'Dar jumped up and ran into the arms of his father.

"It is you!" Acaraho caught him up, being careful not to crush his son in his excitement.

The young man surrendered to his father's embrace.

"Oh, Father, I have missed you so. I am so sorry. I am so sorry," he kept saying.

Acaraho set him back down on the ground and put his hands on Oh'Dar's shoulders, stooping to look him in the eyes.

"Son, do not apologize; everything is alright. I am so glad you are home. Your mother will be beside herself; she never gave up believing you would come back someday."

Oh'Dar hugged Acaraho again, breathing in the familiar scent that represented protection, reassurance, and love.

They walked back to Honovi and Is'Taqa, and Acaraho addressed the Second Chief.

"Please excuse my intrusion; I know your people are not accustomed to the sight of ours, but I could not delay long enough to let you know I was coming here. I hope you can understand."

Then, as Is'Taqa nodded his reassurance, Acaraho turned to Oh'Dar. "Are you ready to come back to Kthama? Or do you want to stay here a while?"

"I am ready to come home."

Turning to Honovi and Is'Taqa, Oh'Dar said, "I will be back after a while. I do want to spend some time with you, but I need to see my mother, Nadi-wani, and my brother."

Acise watched him as he spoke and again as he packed up.

As a courtesy, one of the braves brought Storm

over. The horse bucked at seeing Acaraho, but Oh'Dar was able to quieten him down. He called, and Kweeuu came out of the brush. Then Oh'Dar and Acaraho bade everyone goodbye, and they started on their way to Kthama.

The watchers along the route sent calls and whistles ahead that Acaraho was returning and that he had Oh'Dar and Kweeuu with him. By the time they reached Kthama, the Great Entrance was filled with fidgeting bodies and animated chatter. At the front waited Adia, Nadiwani, Nootau, and Nimida.

Backlit by the sun, which shone through the entrance, the silhouettes of two people, a horse, and a wolf broke through into the cavern.

Adia ran to them, and within moments she and Oh'Dar were in each other's arms, tears running down their faces. Oh'Dar hugged his mother as she sobbed in relief and joy.

Nadiwani and Nootau joined them shortly.

Khon'Tor and Tehya watched from the side. She looked up at Khon'Tor for an explanation. "I will tell you later," he said, eyeing Oh'Dar carefully. *So the Waschini has returned. I did not expect to see him again. Whatever story he has to tell will be of interest to us all.* "It is a long story, but one you should know."

"Look how excited they are," she exclaimed.

Khon'Tor looked over at them as they clamored over each other with wide smiles and much laughter.

She is right. This is of happy significance for Adia and those closest to him.

He addressed Tehya. "I never thought this day would come. Perhaps I will order a celebration."

Tehya smiled and nodded, having no idea how different her mate was from the male he used to be, or how every day he feared losing her.

As they continued to crowd around Oh'Dar to welcome him home, Acaraho signaled for someone to come and help with Storm. The guard unhooked Oh'Dar's travel bags and handed them over before steadying the stallion.

Acaraho looked at the animal as they led him away. He was far larger than the Brothers' ponies and even their horses, and the dark, unbroken coat seemed to shimmer. Though the People did not keep the animals, he did find them beautiful, and this one exceptionally so.

"We have so much to catch up on," said Adia. "I want to hear everything."

"I do, too," said Oh'Dar. "I am sure there have been a lot of changes while I have been gone," and he looked over at Khon'Tor with the unfamiliar young female at his side. "I look forward to hearing all about it. However, I must take care of Storm, and I will see you at the evening meal."

Acaraho and Adia looked at each other happily.

"I will walk part of the way with you and then I

am going on ahead to see that your workshop is freshened and food and water brought in for Kweeuu. I am sure he will stay with you there?" added Acaraho.

The people parted to make way for the High Protector walking with his Waschini son as Kweeuu trotted along beside them.

It was a sight to remember.

Khon'Tor had watched Oh'Dar talking with his family. Like many others, the Leader had expected never to see the offspring again. Only he was not an offspring any longer, in any regard. Wherever he had been, he had come back with confidence that Khon'Tor would never have thought possible. *At the time he left, I was convinced he would bring trouble to us all. But now, after what the High Council Overseer shared, it does not seem the Waschini are our biggest problem. But how can I be sure?*

Khon'Tor looked down at Tehya, who grinned up at him.

During the evening meal, the room was abuzz with conversation. Many came to their table and welcomed Oh'Dar home. His family members had little time to talk with him until much later after most of the others had left. Despite Nadiwani's encouragement, Nimida, whom the Healer's Helper had taken under her wing, did not join them that evening, respecting this reunion as special family time. She remained unaware that she was Nootau's sister, separated from him at birth.

Once they were finally alone together, Adia struggled to think what she wanted to know about first.

"Where have you been, Oh'Dar? Where did you go? Did you find your Waschini family?" She wanted to know everything and all at once.

"Before I tell you all that, did you find my note, and did you understand it?" he asked.

"Yes, we did. At least I think we did. We believed it was saying that you went to find your Waschini family and that we were to let you go," Adia said, then pushed away the painful memory.

"I worried for so long that you would not understand it. That you would think it was easy for me to leave. But it wasn't. It broke my heart, but it was something I had to do," he said.

Adia wanted so much to ask him if it was what Khon'Tor had said to him, about being a threat to the People, that had made him leave. And if so, what had brought him home? But she would get to that later; it was too serious a topic to handle first thing.

"As for your question, yes, I did find them. First, I ended up in a small town, like the Brothers' village, only made of wood structures they call buildings— all straight up and down and harsh angles. We would never construct such things. It seems that little they build blends in with nature," he said.

Adia's heart jumped at his use of the word *we*.

He still thinks of us as his family, his real family.

Oh'Dar explained how the people in the town had taken him in and treated him well, how they had tracked down his original family. They laughed at the story of the Waschini eating-tools, finding the word 'fork' particularly humorous for some reason. He explained about the Waschini concept of money as a means of exchange, and they found it as peculiar as he had. There were so many details to share. He told them about his grandmother and Mr. Jenkins, the stable master. He did not tell them the story about how his uncle had paid some men to murder his mother and father. He would wait for a more appropriate time to share that part.

"So, you must have learned your birth name?" asked Nadiwani.

Oh'Dar smiled.

"Grayson Stone Morgan the Third."

"It has a nice rhythm," said Acaraho.

"Oh, I could talk all night about what went on there. Please, tell me what has been going on *here*? And who is that little, tiny beauty with Khon'Tor?" he asked.

"Oh, there is so much to tell you. I do not know where to start. But for one thing, your father and I are officially paired," put in Adia.

Oh'Dar's face broke into a huge smile, which

quickly turned into a frown. "What? How is that possible? But you are still the Healer are you not, Mama?"

"Oh, yes. No, that has not changed. But the High Council repealed the Second Law forbidding Healers and Helpers to pair. We were joined at the recent Ashwea Awhidi."

Oh'Dar reached across the table and grabbed his mother's hand. Then he looked over at Nootau.

"Are you—did you—" Oh'Dar could not help but be struck by how much Nootau had grown. In their brief exchanges since he had come back, Oh'Dar could see signs of leadership that had surfaced in Nootau. In many ways, they were very much alike; they had both learned from Acaraho how to be expert hunters and providers. Aside from the fact that Oh'Dar could not feel the magnetic currents of Etera, the other area in which they differed was that Nootau had not shown any interest in their mother's trade. Oh'Dar, on the other hand, had been fascinated from the start by the different herbs and concoctions that Adia and Nadiwani prepared. Oh'Dar wondered what was ahead for his younger brother. Would he, at some distant point, replace their father as High Protector? Then, realizing he did not want to think of his parents getting older, nor the fact that, as the People had such long lifespans, they would most likely outlive him, Oh'Dar returned his attention to the conversation.

Nootau smiled and shook his head, no. "I am not

ready. I thought I was, but I am content with waiting a while longer now."

"So tell me, who *is* that with Khon'Tor? Is that his new mate?"

Acaraho spoke this time. "Yes, it is. Her name is Tehya. She is from the People of the Far High Hills. They were also paired at the last Ashwea Awhidi, along with your mother and me. There have been a lot of changes here. For one thing, Khon'Tor is not as you knew him to be. He has changed, and I think I believe it to be genuine."

"For the better? I thought so. Even though I only saw him for a moment, he looked different. More relaxed. Calmer. Softer—if you can use that term in any context with someone of Khon'Tor's personality," he joked. "So, what caused it?"

"It is a long story and not all of it can be told. But suffice it to say that people can change. It often takes a lot—sometimes it takes losing everything someone holds dear—but it can happen. Khon'Tor is living proof of that. Much of the time, you can hardly tell he is the same person," Acaraho explained.

They sat for a while longer before deciding to call it a night. Oh'Dar and Kweeuu left to check on Storm again before going back to his workshop to sleep. The others made their way toward their quarters; Nootau with Nadiwani, and Acaraho with Adia.

Oh'Dar stood in front of his workshop door. He was flooded by bittersweet memories of the last time he was there. Breathing deeply, he pushed the familiar wooden door aside and entered, Kweeuu padding along with him.

It was exactly the same but had recently been cleaned. Fresh flowers lined the room; new herbs had been hung. His sleeping mat, as well as Kweeuu's, had been stuffed with fresh bedding. Kweeuu immediately went over to the food and water bowls, obviously remembering.

Finally alone, Oh'Dar let the feeling of relief flood over him. He was home, and it felt like home. He might not be physically one of the People, but he was in his heart and in their hearts. And that was what mattered.

He plopped down on the sleeping mat and stretched out, surrounded by all the familiar scents. Kweeuu finished eating and came over to stand in front of Oh'Dar.

"Alright, but just for tonight. Come on," and Kweeuu bounded onto Oh'Dar's mat instead of his own—wallowing excitedly over his young master.

Oh'Dar patted Kweeuu and said, "So why did you come to find me? What was that all about? I expected to find some tragedy here, something urgent requiring my attention. But everyone seems fine. My mother and father never seemed happier, and now they are paired. And Nadiwani and Nootau; they seem well. Even Khon'Tor seems to have changed.

He does not seem to be the iron-fisted ruler he used to be. So why? Why did you track me down so far away? Just to bring me back because you wanted me here?"

Kweeuu cocked his head at Oh'Dar, then delivered a big lick across his face.

"I guess you are keeping your secrets to yourself, huh? Well then, let us get some rest."

Oh'Dar wove his fingers through the wolf's thick fur and peered contentedly into the darkness for a while. Then he rolled over and let himself slip off to sleep, enjoying the warmth of Kweeuu curled up next to him.

Acaraho and Adia talked about Oh'Dar for a long time before falling asleep. Adia had never given up hope that Oh'Dar would come home. There was so much ground to cover; she wanted to know everything about her son, what he had seen, learned, and how he had been treated. She wondered if the terrible stories they had heard about the Waschini were true. Mostly she wanted to hear that he had come home because he had realized his place in life was here, and that he was back for good.

CHAPTER 3

The next morning with Tehya in tow, Khon'Tor talked to Mapiya and the other senior females about a celebration for Oh'Dar's return. They had been blessed with a particularly good harvest that year—more than they needed—so he instructed them to put on a generous provision in the young man's honor.

After they left the females, Tehya asked Khon'Tor about Oh'Dar. She had never seen a Waschini before and was fascinated by him. Not a Brother, and yet not one of the People, for sure.

"A long time ago, Tehya, the People's High Council warned us about the Waschini. The stories told about them have not been flattering. We have heard that they are heartless creatures who take what they want without regard for anything or anyone else; they are capable of brutality and sacrilege. We have not heard one positive thing about them.

"However, Oh'Dar is a Waschini. And from the time he came here, he has never caused any trouble. He has willingly learned our ways and customs. He has tried to fit in and belong. There has never been any evidence of cruelty in him—just the opposite. He has consistently demonstrated a kind and generous heart and is as much one of us as is any one of the People.

"I did not always feel this way about him, though. From the time our Healer, Adia, rescued him and brought him here, I believed he was a threat to our people, perhaps even ushering in the Wrak-Ayya. I fought with his mother over him, though at some point, we came to a kind of truce. But I never completely accepted him and was pleased when he left. Now I am not sure that the Waschini will be the cause of our downfall—and for now, I see his return as a great blessing. Especially for Adia. But also for ourselves; no doubt he will teach us a great deal about the Waschini world."

Khon'Tor did not expect Tehya to understand everything but knew that over time she would piece it all together.

"Now, I need to go and talk to Acaraho. In several months the High Council will be reconvening, and we need to make preparations for their return. Do you want to go back and talk to the females?"

"No, I think I will return to our quarters. I am working on a surprise for you."

"Oh? And just what would that be?"

Tehya pursed her lips and pretended to scowl. "Now, if I told you that, then it would not be much of a surprise, would it?" she laughed.

"You could at least give me a hint," he said.

"No, no hints, Adoeete. You will just have to wait and see."

"All right then. Go ahead and tease me. I will catch up with you later." Making sure that no one was around, he gave her a playful swat on the rear as she left, which made her turn back and wag her finger at him.

Khon'Tor took a moment to enjoy watching her walk away.

I do not deserve to be this happy. By what grace and mercy have I been blessed to have this innocent, loving female for my own? So far, none of my other appetites have returned—though I do so enjoy her submissiveness.

Acaraho and Khon'Tor sat in a meeting room with Mapiya, who had become the female's informal coordinator.

"The High Council Overseer has sent word that the High Council will return next mid-summer to discuss further the several topics it introduced at the Ashea Awhidi. Though this will be nowhere as complicated as the Ashwea Awhidi, we will still have a sizeable group to house. The High Council is asking that not only the Leaders of each community come, but also the Healers and the Healer's Helpers. No doubt they will bring some number of assistants with them, though these will, of course, not be involved in the meetings," Khon'Tor explained.

Acaraho continued, "I will take care of the meeting areas and escorts and establish the routes for the guards and watchers. Even though there will not be as many people, some logistics remain the same. Mapiya, I will be glad if you will help me with preparing the living quarters once we agree on them and I have mapped them out, and if you would arrange food preparation with the females, as you did before."

"It is still quite a way off, but it is beneficial for our people to have something to look forward to. Once we have completed our initial planning, we will not need to meet again for some time," said Khon'Tor.

Mapiya nodded. She had her complement of helpers selected, and though it was still a way off, as Khon'Tor had said, the anticipation was already creating a murmur of excitement. Even though the purpose of the visit would not be known to most, receiving guests always raised the energy, regardless. Visitors meant a chance to socialize and hear what was going on in the other communities.

Khon'Tor dismissed Mapiya so he and Acaraho could talk alone.

"Since you have said nothing, High Protector, I assume no reports have come back from the scouting groups about any other communities." It was a statement, not a question.

"Correct. The first I sent out are by now just reaching the outer edge of our territory. I do not expect to hear back from them for several months yet. It is a great deal of ground to cover. The group covering the closer areas could have a report as soon as the end of snowfall. I doubt we will know much by the time of the High Council meeting. Other communities may have the same problem—there is a great deal of ground to cover, and the Sarnonn are said to be masters at hiding."

"I wish I had a better feeling about this," Khon Tor offered. "The challenge is daunting. Not only to find pockets of our people which we have not before encountered but also to find the Sarnonn if they even exist—and we have no proof of that—and somehow solicit their cooperation?"

The old Khon'Tor would never have admitted a weakness. He has changed, thought Acaraho. *I have heard of this before—sometimes going through a traumatic experience changes people. He came close, so very close to losing everything. For any Leader to have his position stripped from him in shame would cut to the core, but even more so for an Alpha like him. And until Adia saved him by withdrawing her accusation, he stood at the precipice of banishment—the worse punishment possible. So I have to consider that he has genuinely changed. And if I wholly believed in such things, I would think it possible we could even become allies. But I know that even Adia is not completely convinced that the old Khon'Tor is gone for good. Changes do not always hold up over time.*

"We have several months. We need to gather all the information we can before picking a path. Perhaps the other communities will have encouraging news even if we do not," said Acaraho, returning to the moment at hand.

Khon'Tor looked at Acaraho and shifted the conversation, "How is he doing?"

Acaraho knew he meant Oh'Dar.

"He appears to be strong and healthy. We talked a long time into the dark last night, but not about anything in much depth. We know he has been with the Waschini all these years. He told us what it was like and how differently from our ways they live. It is possible he will be able to help us understand them better. His mother, of course, is beside herself with joy at his return," said Acaraho, making a goodwill offering of disclosure.

"All this time worrying about the Waschini when we ourselves are the threat," mused Khon'Tor.

"We do not know if the Waschini may be a problem. We just know that right now, they are not at the forefront of our concerns." Then Acaraho added, "You have led us through some serious challenges in the past Khon'Tor. You will lead us through whatever lies ahead."

"If I have, it has been by the grace of the Great Spirit. I have made many mistakes. Terrible decisions. I have done things that haunt me to this day. Things for which payment will one day come due—" Khon'Tor's voice trailed off.

He finally continued. "From the beginning, I believed Oh'Dar presented a serious threat to our Community, perhaps even ushering in the Wrak-Ayya. Now I believe I was wrong about that."

Acaraho patiently listened while Khon'Tor spoke. He had made a commitment to Adia to nurture the new peace between the three of them. If she could forgive Khon'Tor for what he did to her, he also had to do his best, but he did not have to like it. The Leaders' personal problems had affected the community far too long. The People needed unity and cooperation, not more of the division and animosity that had tainted the past.

He was glad to hear that Khon'Tor's perceptions of Oh'Dar had apparently changed, but was disturbed by the Leader's other remarks.

Khon'Tor looked at Acaraho and nodded. "Keep me informed."

The Leader got up and headed for the door, but before he exited, he turned back slightly, and without making eye contact, he announced, "I have decided to hold a celebration in honor of Oh'Dar's return. Please tell Adia."

Khon'Tor left the meeting room but did not go anywhere in particular. There was nothing he had to attend to for the rest of the day. He took a circuitous route to the outside and went for a long walk down the winding paths surrounding Kthama.

As he walked, he reminisced about the last time he had faced the High Council. The one where Adia had given him back his life. She had called for a hearing to turn him in for his violation of her, but when the High Council decided to banish him, she had vehemently admonished them. Then she had withdrawn her accusation. Once an accusation was withdrawn, it could not be brought again.

In effect, she had taken away all their power to punish him in the matter. Khon'Tor could never be brought up again for his crimes against Adia.

All the years of suffering I caused her. And in the end, Adia freed me. If it were not for her, I would be wandering alone out here, banished, trying to scrape out an existence. But what of the others? I hurt more than just her. At some point, my debt will come due. And not even Adia can protect me from that. How unfortunate that the female from the Far High Hills, whom I also took Without Her Consent, ended up being paired with the watcher, Akule. Her presence is a constant reminder of my transgressions. She keeps her eyes from me, no doubt denying my existence, and she has maintained her silence —but for how long?

He thought back to when he was talking about Oh'Dar with Awan and had turned to see that the offspring had overheard their conversation. He wondered if Adia knew; if now that he was back, Oh'Dar had told them what had probably caused him to go. Khon'Tor was fairly confident his remark had driven Oh'Dar to leave, but he hoped Adia did not know. The peace between them freed him to focus on his true responsibility, which was to be the Leader of the People of the High Rocks, as Chief Ogima had admonished him to be.

As Khon'Tor passed the area where he had raped the nameless female at the last Ashwea Awhidi, he wondered what had become of her. She had no way of knowing who he was, as he had worn a hood, and luckily the males from the High Red Rocks were as large as him, so his physical build had not given away his identity. But he had no idea who she was, either. Wherever she had come from, she had returned there changed forever.

If I could undo what I have done, I would. I will have to live with it, just as they do, for the rest of my days. I cannot change it, and I cannot make it right. Only the Great Spirit knows when the day of restitution will come for me.

Khon'Tor continued, deep in thought until finally he stopped and looked around. Unconsciously, he had come to the area where Hakani had taken her own life. He could see her standing near the edge of the path, holding the helpless, screaming offspring,

Nootau. He remembered her ramblings about Adia being his First Choice, how no female would ever accept him again, how she would take both his offspring to their deaths with her—Nootau in her arms, and the other she claimed was newly growing inside her. Then, finally, her brisk turn to step over the edge into the waters below. Khon'Tor could feel Acaraho standing over him—enraged, canines revealed—knowing that he was seconds from death. And then he thought back again to the High Council meeting when Adia had taken the power away from the High Council and masterfully ended the battle between them. Somehow, all of this had worked together to create in him a new male—or maybe it had broken down the stronghold that had prevented him from being that male all along.

Khon'Tor reached down and selected a smooth, brown rock from those at his feet. He fingered it a moment, lost in thought, and then tossed it far out over the edge, watching it drop to the waters below, as had Hakani.

I am not sorry you took your own life, but I do some-times wonder if you found peace in your return to the Mother.

Khon'Tor turned to go back to Kthama and Tehya and happened to look down. There, in striking contrast to the rocky dirt path, rested a single beauti-ful, pure white feather. Not one for signs—he left those to the Healers—he still felt compelled to pick it up. *Here, at this place, in the midst of all these painful memories and the ugliness that life can be, to find such a creation of beauty is truly a gift.*

Tehya was struggling to find her place at the High Rocks. She had not expected to be the center of attention everywhere she went. When she was with Khon'Tor, she was content; she looked forward to being with him. It was filling the time in between that was the problem.

Sitting at the worktable in the Leader's Quarters, she sighed.

I have to find my place here. I have to be more than Khon'Tor's mate. If I build my life around him alone, I will come to resent every time that he is called away. I wish someone had prepared me for this. I never seriously considered the possibility of being paired to a Leader, and I must force myself to come out of my shell somehow. I am Third Rank now. I must become stronger.

She had heard stories about his first mate, Hakani, that she was overbearing and that there seemed little peace between her and Khon'Tor. She had also overheard talk about the long-standing animosity between Hakani and the Healer, Adia. Tehya had met Adia several times and found her friendly and easy-going enough, so she thought that the problem must have lain with Hakani. She knew there was more to the story, but being so isolated, she had little chance to learn it.

I need to make friends with some of the females here. I cannot rely on Khon'Tor to fill my world. I am expected to be a Leader, Third Rank, and I do not want to let him down.

Tehya looked for her wraps and selected one of her favorites. Though the other females wore cover-ups, due to her lighter coloring it was even more important for her modesty to do so. And in truth, she enjoyed picking from an array of items to wear, just as she enjoyed occasionally plaiting her hair. Happy with her selection, Tehya headed out to find the Healer.

Adia was walking with Oh'Dar when Tehya found her.

"Good morning, Adia," she began.

"Good morning, Tehya," replied Adia. "Have you met my son, Oh'Dar? He just returned from a long absence," and she turned to Oh'Dar.

"No, I have not, but I was there when you arrived. Everyone is so glad to see you again. I am looking forward to getting to know you." Oh'Dar was the first Waschini she had ever seen. She could not stop looking at his smooth, terribly pale skin, straight black hair, and his striking blue eyes.

"I see that you wear coverings, but yours are more intricate than most worn by females here," said Oh'Dar. "I would be glad to show you the skins I have in my workshop, and I could make you some new ones," he volunteered.

Tehya relaxed a bit, thinking perhaps he understood what it was like to be an outsider. Grateful for his kindness, she developed an immediate affinity for this stranger.

"Oh, I would appreciate that very much. I already have an idea I want to try out, but I am having difficulty with it. Perhaps you could help?"

"Oh'Dar is great with new ideas, and he is skilled with fine crafts. It is because of him that we have the large water-tight baskets hanging in the living quarters. It has saved us all numerous daily trips to the Mother Stream," offered Adia.

"I would be glad to help you with your idea. Let us go after the meal, and you can tell me what you have in mind."

"You are welcome to eat with us if you wish," the Healer suggested.

Tehya nodded gratefully and followed them to the eating area. She could not stop staring at Oh'Dar. He was much shorter than the People and had no down covering over his body, which she realized accounted for his heavier wrappings. He could almost be mistaken for one of the Brothers, except that his blue eyes made it an impossibility. Other than a slight impediment, maybe due to his lack of sharp canines, he spoke like one of the People, although his Handspeak was more eloquent and fluid than theirs.

Passing through, Khon'Tor spotted his mate sitting with the Healer and Oh'Dar. He came over and stood behind Tehya, placing a hand on each of her shoulders while he spoke with Adia and Oh'Dar. Tehya reached up and affectionately placed her hands on his.

"I see you have met my mate, Tehya."

"Yes, we have. Oh'Dar is going to help her with —" started Adia.

"Sshh! It is a surprise," exclaimed Tehya, smiling.

"Oh!" Oh'Dar grinned in return.

"Yes. So I have been told," Khon'Tor said. "Well, I can see you are all up to no good, so I will leave you to your day."

Tehya smiled tauntingly up at her mate.

Turning to her, he said, "Please let me know if you prefer we eat alone tonight or if you would rather eat here with the community."

Tehya wanted to eat in their quarters, but considering she had just decided to participate more, she said she wished to eat with the others.

"Very well, then. I will find you later. Adia—"

Adia looked up at him.

"Did Acaraho tell you about my decision to hold a celebration for Oh'Dar's return?"

Adia shook her head, no.

"He will tell you when I have settled on the time."

And then Khon'Tor nodded to the others and left.

Oh'Dar looked at his mother, then at Tehya. "Forgive me speaking so personally about your mate, Tehya, but Khon'Tor is very different. He has changed a great deal."

"I take no offense. I have heard he used to be more—standoffish? Highly-strung? But this is the only way I have known him to be," she replied.

"We are fortunate to have him as a Leader," said Adia. "We are the largest community we know of, and it is not easy to lead so many. If the turbulent times of the Wrak-Ayya are coming, his leadership will become even more critical. He is also an eloquent speaker. You have not yet had the opportunity to hear him address all of us at once." Then she added, "Tehya, how are you adjusting?"

"I miss home and my parents. But each day it gets easier."

"If you need someone to talk to, I hope you will consider coming to me," said Adia.

Tehya smiled her thanks, and after they had finished eating, Oh'Dar led Tehya off to see his workshop.

Tehya looked around the spacious room. The chalked walls brightened everything considerably. She took in the overhead log beams, which she imagined were for hanging items that needed to dry. In one corner stood a structure similar to those used to stretch hides back at the Far High Hills. Behind some large tables in the back were two stacks of hides and furs. She flipped through them, admiring each one. The furs were too heavy for her use at present, but she thought them beautiful.

"Do you see anything you can use?" Oh'Dar asked, waiting for her to examine everything to her satisfaction.

"The skins and furs are beautiful," she said, running her fingers through them, "and I think they would be so very perfect for the colder weather. But, for my surprise, I need something much more light-weight than anything I see here."

"I can get some woven cotton fabric from the Brothers. Would that be more to your liking?"

"Oh, yes. I just need something lightweight enough to—" her voice trailed off.

"No need to be embarrassed Tehya, I understand the concept of needing wrappings. After all, I am more like the Brothers than the People, as you can see." He opened his arms with a little bow as if to put himself on display, making her laugh.

He is very kind. Not at all like the stories Khon'Tor has told me of the Waschini.

"It is nice to see another of the People wearing coverings. I have had to all my life because Kthama is too cold for me. And of course, the Brothers do. But in my experience, your wrappings are more elaborate than most of those worn by any females here, and definitely more so than those the Elders wear. Perhaps you will start a new trend," he laughed. "I see no reason why males cannot also wear wraps."

"I would love to have something made out of these. They are so beautiful. But I definitely need something more delicate for what I am planning right now," she said.

"Well, it is settled then. I am sure the Brothers have some lightweight fabrics that are just what you are looking for.

"Oh. that would be so kind."

"It is settled then. I need to go back anyway, and I will bring what I can. What is the surprise you want to make?"

Tehya blushed visibly.

"Oh, I am sorry, I did not mean to pry. Well, just let me know if there is any other way I can help you."

Tehya thanked Oh'Dar. She wondered if she might one day be able to visit the Brothers and decided to ask Khon'Tor if she could, even though Oh'Dar had not offered. *This was a good day,* she decided. *Maybe I have made another friend!*

That evening, when they were alone in the Leader's Quarters, Tehya approached Khon'Tor about the possibility of going sometime to the Brothers' village with Oh'Dar.

Khon'Tor closed his eyes and took a moment before answering. *I can see by her excitement that this is something she truly wants to do. How could I tell her no; she never asks for anything for herself.*

"You would not be able to make the trip there

and back in one day. If the Brothers are comfortable with it, you may go someday, yes. I do not believe they would have a problem being visited by such a very small person. But when that time comes, I will have Acaraho send guards with you. And alert the watchers along the way to closely monitor your journey. And if you were not back in three days' time, I would come to look for you myself."

Tehya jumped up and hugged Khon'Tor and thanked him profusely. Solemnly, he watched her bounce with joy around the room.

I would keep her locked up in here safely forever if I could. In truth, I hope she forgets about the idea.

Adia had found Acaraho and asked about Khon'Tor's decision to hold a celebration. "I am a little shocked that he is going to commemorate Oh'Dar's return. I think that would be—I do not know what to say—"

"There seems to be little left of the monster who —" It was Acaraho's turn for his voice to trail off.

"It is alright. You can say it. There is power in spoken truth. He is nothing like he was when he attacked me decades ago. It is true, Acaraho. And I believe it is likely genuine. If I did not, I would be very worried for Tehya. As it is, I am keeping my senses attuned to any change, for her sake as well as ours. I can only hope it holds up."

"It is for the best of all of us as well as for him,"

said Acaraho. "I am not sure what made the difference, but I believe it was your defense of him at the High Council."

"I think that was part of it. But I think there was more. Perhaps he just hit rock bottom. Perhaps he was sick of the fighting. If you remember, he admitted to everything and did not offer any defense —even when facing banishment. And I think Tehya plays a part. There is something innocent and trusting about her. In every way, she is the opposite of what Hakani was. So I think it was a combination of factors coming together at the perfect time in the perfect way."

"Well, for your sake, I am trying to put what he did to you behind us and believe that the change is real. And for Tehya's sake, I wish them the best."

"I do too. And I hope she will give him lots of little Khon'Tors," added Adia.

"Oh, by the Spirit, I do not know about that!"

They both laughed.

"I will tell you as soon as the plans for the assembly are finalized," and Acaraho squeezed her hand before he left.

After Acaraho had left, Adia considered what they had discussed. *I do not want to doubt that Khon'Tor has changed. He has a new attitude toward Oh'Dar, too. But I cannot forget what Hakani said about his torturing her. Was that another of her lies? Tehya seems genuinely happy. Only time will tell, and I will keep my senses open.*

Acise was helping her mother gather some of the harvest. Her thoughts kept returning to Oh'Dar. She loved her memories of when he had brought shells and colorful stones to her, and his sitting with them at the evening fires. He was always kind to her, and she had felt like his sister. But she was not feeling sisterly toward him now.

"Momma, when do you think Oh'Dar will come back?"

Honovi replied without looking up from her work as she sorted the roots she had gathered, "I am not sure. Are you anxious for him to return?"

"Oh, yes. Momma, you know how he used to bring me shells and agates. And he used to kid around with Snana and me. Chasing us, jumping in leaf piles. We loved it when he visited." She paused before continuing, "He seems to have changed a lot in such a short time."

"So have you. That is how it is. It seems that one day your children are happily playing in the mud and the next—"

Honovi stopped and straightened up, placing her hands on her hips and looking at her daughter. "Acise, do you find Oh'Dar attractive? I mean, do you think he is handsome, even though he is pure Waschini?"

"Well, you can hardly tell he is Waschini, Momma. He is lighter-skinned, but if it were not for those blue eyes, he does not look that much different from you or me. After all, I am a quarter Waschini, though I seldom think about it. Grandmother was a Brother, and I guess I came out favoring her side, as you did.

"I remember Papa teaching Oh'Dar to hunt; he is skilled with the bow. And he rides as well as any of the braves, maybe almost as well as Pajackok!"

Honovi paused a moment. *I do not remember my daughter's eyes lighting up when she is speaking of Pajackok as they do when it is Oh'Dar.* She went back to her task, making a note to speak with Is'Taqa about this later. Up to now, Honovi had thought her daughter favored Pajackok and that their eventual bonding was a given.

Sooner than expected, within a few days, Oh'Dar returned to the Brothers.

Honovi was the first to greet him. "I am pleased to see you have returned so soon."

"It is good to be here; I miss you all. I have also come on a mission. I want to trade for some of your cotton weavings. I need some lighter weight material than the skins and hides I have."

Hearing Oh'Dar's voice, Acise came out of the shelter and joined them. She tried to pay attention to what they were saying but kept stealing looks at Oh'Dar.

"When do you have to return? Surely you are at least staying for the night?" asked Honovi.

"Yes, please; the trip here and back takes a while."

"Give me a moment to put together a selection of fabrics and then join me in the shelter."

As her mother walked away, Acise finally found her voice.

"Oh'Dar, remember the trinkets you used to bring me?"

"Of course. And I also remember you throwing them at me!"

"Oh, yes. Well, I guess I did." She lowered her eyes and smiled. "I have quite a collection now and have found another great place to find them since you left. Maybe I can show it to you some time."

Is'Taqa watched the interaction between the two, making a note to speak with Honovi about it later.

For much of the rest of the day, Oh'Dar and Honovi went through her collection of woven fabrics from which Oh'Dar picked out several colors that he believed would appeal to Tehya.

Later, Oh'Dar and Is'Taqa spent some time discussing the horses and ponies, while Acise followed them around as Kweeuu had done when he was a cub.

Later that evening, they chatted around the fire. Oh'Dar knew the time would come when questions would begin in earnest, but the mood was not yet right. Finally, they turned in, and as before, there was more than enough room for all of them in the family shelter.

Oh'Dar was tired and would not have awoken during the night were it not for someone snuggling up next to him and slipping her hand gently into his. In his dazed state, he startled. He turned his head enough to see Acise looking at him in the dim light. She smiled and then closed her eyes and went back to sleep, leaving her fingers intertwined in his.

Oh'Dar waited until her breathing slowed and gently removed his hand. Rolling over, he turned his back to her sleeping form, careful not to wake Honovi and a bit taken aback at Acise's forward behavior.

He did not sleep for the rest of the night.

Oh'Dar returned to Kthama the next day with his selection of fabrics for Tehya. After letting the others know of his return, he and Tehya went directly to Oh'Dar's workshop to start working on her idea. Honovi had so many beautiful dyes—shades of color Tehya had never seen before. Oh'Dar happily watched her face light up when she saw them.

As she was finishing up going through them, Oh'Dar released an overhead basket that contained a selection of fine bone needles wrapped in a pouch, and brought it down for her to select from. But instead of being interested in the needles, she was more intrigued by the knot that had secured the basket.

"How did you tie that? The one you just released with one pull?" she asked. Oh'Dar took a strand of sinew and showed her. She smiled profusely with a twinkle in her eye.

"Oh'Dar, that is all I needed. Do you mind if I stay here and work on my idea by myself? It is a little personal," and she blushed.

"No, of course not. Take all the time you need. You are welcome to use any of the supplies here at any time. I can always get more, and I am glad to help you. And I also hope that you—or *whoever*—enjoys your surprise," Oh'Dar smiled back with a twinkle in his eye. After Tehya had shushed him in the eating area the other day, it was obvious that the surprise had something to do with Khon'Tor.

Oh'Dar surrendered his workshop to Tehya and left her to play with her designs.

As he walked away, he realized how much he was still distracted by Acise's actions of the night before. She was no longer the little girl he had played with years ago or the older girl he had thought of as a sister. She was now a beautiful woman with her mother's kind heart. But it was a complication he did not need. He still did not know where he belonged, and he could not let his heart get in his way as it had with his first teacher, Miss Blain. *Grandmother is right;*

there is lots of time to be paired, and I need to stay my
course. But just what is my course?

Acaraho was sitting with Mapiya discussing Khon'-
Tor's ideas for Oh'Dar's celebration when they were
interrupted by Akule entering the work area.

"Commander Acaraho. I need a word with you."
Acaraho rose and walked away with Akule. Out of
earshot, he asked what the interruption was about.

"One of the outposted watchers has returned
with news of what they think might mean there is an
undiscovered establishment relatively close."

"An establishment of the People?" asked Acaraho.
After Akule had answered and left the room,
Acaraho sat in silence.

Khon'Tor entered the Leader's Quarters to find them
empty. His eyes swept the room, and he was about to
leave when he heard a small chuckle escape from
under the sleeping covers. He pretended not to
notice and walked about the room a bit. Within a
moment, another laugh escaped. He walked over to
the bed and quickly threw back the covers. There lay
Tehya with a particularly large smile on her face.

"Are you hiding from me?" he asked, pleased at
her playfulness.

"No, I wanted to surprise you!"

"If you wanted to surprise me, you should have kept quiet."

"Well, hiding is not my surprise. But this is!" and she hopped up off the mat and came over to stand in front of him, spinning to let him see her new wrappings.

"Are those new?" he asked, running his gaze over the brightly colored wraps that loosely covered her figure.

"Yes, but that is not the surprise either. Try to keep up! Here, let me show you."

She took hold of a loose bit of tie and slowly pulled it, releasing the front of her top—which parted and fell away, exposing her pert mounds.

"That is—very nice," Khon'Tor smiled, feeling himself respond to her. Her light down did little to cover her details as it did for females with darker coloring.

Tehya gave him her teasing smile and said, "I know you struggle with my wrappings, and I wanted to make it easier for you to remove them. You know, considering how much older you are than I am, Adoeete. I did not want you to tire out before you could get them off me—"

Khon'Tor laughed, "Oh, I can see we have a misunderstanding," and he quickly swept her up and tossed her over his shoulder. "*Old*? *Tired out*? I will show you how old I am and how quickly I tire out."

He carted her back to the sleeping mat while she

laughingly pounded his back with her fists and kicked her feet in mock protest. True to his threat, he took a very long time with her, bringing her to the crest then denying her what she needed over and over until she begged him for release.

"Not until I say so, my love," he whispered in her ear as he expertly brought her to the edge again, then stopped.

"Khon'Tor, please, oh please!"

"No. Not until I give permission."

He teased her again, bringing her to the brink of the splendor and then pausing.

"*Adoeete*," she pleaded, her nails digging into his biceps.

Her begging broke his control, and he could hold himself back no longer. Her submission to his orders excited him even more than had overpowering Hakani.

"As you wish, little Saraste'," he whispered in her ear. He then brushed his lips against hers, moving as he knew she needed to reach completion. She arched her back and cried out as wave after wave of pleasure swallowed her in ecstasy.

He collapsed off her and rolled off to the side as they each took a moment to catch their breath. She laced her fingers through his as they lay next to each other.

It was the last completely carefree evening they would enjoy together for a long while.

There was not a lot of time. Acaraho paced around the small meeting room that Khon'Tor usually claimed as his own. He had to go to Khon'Tor, but he first needed time to think. It was hardly possible that the watcher could be wrong, but if not, then everything was about to change and possibly not for the better.

Before creating such alarm Acaraho wanted to talk to the original watcher who had made the report. He decided to do so after Oh'Dar's celebration.

Unfortunately, time would run out before Acaraho could execute his plan.

CHAPTER 4

Late in the day, everyone was in the Great Chamber waiting for the celebration to begin. The females had outdone themselves in preparing a variety of foodstuffs. Voices were raised in gaiety and lightheartedness. Oh'Dar and his family sat near the platform, knowing Khon'Tor wanted to bring them up to the front at the start of his speech. Tehya joined them at their table as she had taken to doing when she and Khon'Tor were not eating together.

Khon'Tor entered the room, and all eyes followed him to the front, his easy strides and his riveting muscular build as always commanding attention. He turned and raised his hand as he customarily did to signal that he was ready to address them. But before he could begin, Akule came running into the Great Chamber, out of breath.

Khon'Tor paused and Acaraho turned to see

Akule at the back of the room, gasping, his brow furrowed, uncertain at to whether or not he should approach. Acaraho rose and went to speak to the watcher. Khon'Tor was right behind him, leaving the platform at the front of the room.

"What is it, Akule?" asked Khon'Tor quietly.

"Adik'Tar, First Guard Awan told me to come as fast as I could— We have visitors. There are three— figures—approaching Kthama."

"Three figures? What are you talking about? Are these People? Brothers? Waschini?"

"At least one appears to be— A Sarnonn. That is, according to what we believe they looked like. The others—"

Khon'Tor looked at Acaraho, motioned to Adia to move to the front and take over the celebration, and then both males quickly exited the room with Akule. The People started murmuring among themselves.

Adia stood up quickly and addressed the crowd, "Please, go ahead and eat. I am sure it is a matter easily discharged, and we will be back in a moment." And with that, she got up and followed the three males. Concerned, Nadiwani, Nootau, Oh'Dar, and Tehya were not far behind.

Khon'Tor, Acaraho, and Akule arrived at the Great Entrance just as the three figures came through the opening. They were back-lit by Etera's sun, now setting behind them. The largest was huge and was supporting one of the others on his arm. Acaraho signaled for his guards, and within moments the Great Entrance was filled with burly males. As the guards entered, Acaraho saw his family, with Tehya a little way behind.

The High Protector turned back, and now not directly facing the glare, could see the three figures more clearly. He shook his head. *Oh no,* he said under his breath. Then he walked over to Khon'Tor and placed a hand on the Leader's shoulder. Khon'Tor looked briefly at Acaraho, recognizing the sign of support offered by the High Protector.

The first figure before them was clearly a Sarnonn male. Beyond the smaller figure he supported was a third, still shorter.

Acaraho turned back to look at Adia, who stood frozen, one hand covering her mouth and the other instinctively reaching back for Nootau and Oh'Dar. He motioned toward them, and within moments Awan had the family surrounded by guards.

Then he saw Tehya walk unthinkingly over to join Khon'Tor. He signaled again, and another compliment of guards moved to protect her. Khon'Tor turned and strode back to Tehya.

Looking directly at his mate, he said, "You are to go back to our quarters with these guards. Stay there until I return. You are not to leave for any reason."

"Khon'Tor," she started to protest.

"There will be no argument in this matter. Now *go*."

Her eyes widened, and she tried to push back her reaction at the harsh tone he had used with her.

Khon'Tor turned to the guards, "Allow no harm to come to her. If you fail, your lives will be what I make of them."

Seeing Tehya's distress, Oh'Dar asked, "May I go with her?"

Khon'Tor looked over at Acaraho, who nodded his agreement.

The Leader raised his hand, signaling his approval, and Oh'Dar ran to catch up with Tehya, surrounded by her protective wall of guards.

After making sure Tehya was leaving, Khon'Tor walked over to the strangers.

As he sidestepped away from the glare, they became clearly visible. The Sarnonn towered over both Khon'Tor and Acaraho. His shoulders were wider than two of Acaraho's largest guards standing side by side, and his hands and feet were thick and broad. He was covered entirely in heavy dark fur, which had an almost iridescent quality. His dark, deep-set eyes were fixed on Khon'Tor.

As Khon'Tor looked at the figure next in line, the floor shifted under his feet. Supported by the Sarnonn's arm, though obviously ill, was a perfect copy of himself. Same build, same height, the same shock of silver hair on his head. Had it not been for the silver hair, it could have been Nootau. The truth began to dawn on Khon'Tor.

With his heart pounding, he forced his eyes to the last figure in line. He caught his breath as he recognized his first mate, Hakani.

This cannot be happening. Older and heavier, and despite those fur wraps she is wearing, I can tell it is her.

Moments passed.

Finally, Khon'Tor remembered who he was and took a step toward the Sarnonn. "I am Khon'Tor, Leader of the People of the High Rocks. What is your business here?"

The Sarnonn looked Khon'Tor directly in the eye and signed, "I am Haan. I am here to request help for my family." His signing was more clumsy than that of the People or the Brothers and was at first difficult to understand.

Family? Is he saying they are his family? The Sarnonn lacked the digital dexterity of the People, but that seemed clear enough. Khon'Tor knew he had not misunderstood. *The Sarnonn is claiming these two as his family. And he is asking me for help.*

Adia stepped away from her circle of guards. Acaraho bristled as he watched his mate approach the three figures. As she moved forward, she signed to the Sarnonn, "I am Adia. I am the Healer here. What help do you need?"

The Sarnonn nodded to the others and signed clumsily again, "My son is very sick. Please help him." He motioned to the young male, the image of Khon'Tor, whom he was supporting.

Adia looked over at Acaraho for his permission. Acaraho nodded slightly and joined her. Two guards also came forward. Adia put her hand on the young male's forehead. She turned to Nadiwani, "He is burning with fever."

In what appeared to be an act of abject courage, she placed her hand on the Sarnonn's arm and told him in simple signs to help him understand more easily, "We will help you."

Acaraho caught his breath. "*By the Mother, Adia,*" he whispered. It was all he could do not to snatch her hand away. Then he signaled for the guards to take the sick male to her quarters.

Before she left to go and tend to the sick male, Adia looked at the female, Hakani. The last time she had seen her, Hakani was standing on the edge of a drop-off, holding Adia's tiny son, Nootau, intending to kill him along with herself. The Healer was flooded with emotions she had no time to deal with at the moment.

Thought to be dead all these years, Hakani had returned to Kthama. But not alone. She had returned with a Sarnonn and a young male who was undeniably Khon'Tor's son.

Nootau and Nadiwani went with Adia, leaving Acaraho and Khon'Tor alone with the Sarnonn and Hakani.

Khon'Tor struggled for composure. Finally, he looked at Hakani, "What are *your* intentions here?"

Hakani took a step toward him.

Khon'Tor raised his hand abruptly. "*No.*"

Hakani stopped but said, "Believe me, I am more surprised to see you still here as Leader than you are to see me standing before you now. But maybe it is for the better because I need help for Akar'Tor. Your son, Khon'Tor. Akar'Tor is your son."

Khon'Tor turned his head away and ran his hand through the silver crown of his hair, the same streak that singled out Akar'Tor.

My son. The offspring she claimed she was carrying when she stepped over the edge to her death. Somehow she lived. They both lived. But how?

"You will need a place to stay while he recovers," and Khon'Tor raised his hand. Acaraho stepped forward, addressing both the Sarnonn and Hakani.

"I will make arrangements for quarters for you while—the young male—recovers. Please wait here a moment." Acaraho stepped away to speak with Mapiya, who was watching from the very back of the Great Entrance.

Khon'Tor took advantage of those few moments to collect himself.

"Hakani, we looked for you. Acaraho sent parties out to search for you."

"I will tell you all about it, Khon'Tor, but first give us time to recover. It has been a tiresome journey here."

Khon'Tor pulled himself together; he was the Leader of the People of the High Rocks, and he must not let Hakani rattle him, dead or alive.

"Acaraho will take care of your needs. Stay in your quarters until further notice. I will make sure you are informed of your son's progress, and we will send food to you. Allow us, too, this time to adjust to the situation."

He was not sure how much the Sarnonn understood but left that to Hakani to explain to him.

Having spoken with both Mapiya and First Guard Awan, Acaraho returned, also using simple signals to convey his message, "Please go with these males. They will take you to where you can stay and will bring you food. We shall talk more tomorrow. In the meantime, get some rest while our Healer cares for the young male."

The giant appeared to understand and nodded and signed, *"Thank you."*

The guards, followed by Mapiya, led the Sarnonn and Hakani away from the Great Entrance. Acaraho had instructed the guards to take a circuitous route until the community could be told what had happened.

Chatter from the main eating area filtered through to the Great Entrance.

Acaraho spoke. "We need to get back to the assembly, Khon'Tor. For what it is worth, I am sorry. The watcher alerted me last night that these people were in our area. I had my fears but could not be certain—"

"There is no need to apologize. No one could have foreseen this. But let us make it quick; I wish to check on my ma—Tehya. Post extra guards at whatever living quarters you are putting them in, though I am not sure how many we would need should that—Haan—decide to turn on us. I know, everything we believe about them implies that they are peaceful, but—"

"I will take care of it, Adik'Tar," replied Acaraho. "And though it will perhaps be alarming to the community, I suggest we arm them with spears. I will do some drills with them as well."

Khon'Tor and Acaraho returned to the assembly. Khon'Tor walked to the front of the room and raised his hand to speak.

"I called you here tonight to celebrate the return of one of our own, Oh'Dar, son of Adia, the Healer. Unfortunately, an urgent matter has arisen that shortens our celebration. I see that you have eaten, so I will bid you goodnight. However, tomorrow before high sun, I will ask you to assemble again so that I may apprise you of the situation. Enjoy the rest of your evening; Oh'Dar has come home, and this is a time to celebrate."

Khon'Tor lowered his hand and walked out of the Great Chamber.

Acaraho went to find Adia and Nadiwani while Khon'Tor went directly to his quarters to speak with Tehya.

Oh'Dar accompanied Tehya to the Leader's Quarters, and the guards waited in the corridor. Once inside, Tehya paced around the room.

"What is going on, Oh'Dar? Who are those people? And why was Khon'Tor so cross with me?" She was distraught, and though she was fighting them, tears were threatening to course down her cheeks.

"Tehya, he was only cross because he was concerned for your safety. He did not have time to explain things, and he needed you to do as he said."

"Who was that—*monster*?"

"Yes, I know, I have never seen a Sarnonn before, either. I heard they were larger than the People, but it is hard to take in. I do not think anyone believed they still existed. But for now, you need to calm down. There is nothing for you to worry about."

Suppressing his own reaction to the sight of a

Sarnonn, Oh'Dar went over to the eating area and
moistened a Catalpa leaf.

"Here, go and lie down and rest with this on your
forehead. I will stay until Khon'Tor arrives."

Tehya did as he said and Oh'Dar sat a distance
away in the eating area, wondering what was going
on back in the Great Entrance.

It was not long before the creaking of the wooden
door being opened announced Khon'Tor's arrival. He
nodded to Oh'Dar at the eating table, and then his
gaze found Tehya lying asleep across the room.

Oh'Dar got up to leave, but before he could,
Khon'Tor stopped him and signed, "Thank you for
staying with her."

Oh'Dar nodded and quietly left.

Khon'Tor went to Tehya and stretched out beside
her, trying not to wake her, but she felt the mat shift
under his weight and opened her eyes to meet his.
She immediately wrapped her arms around him.
Khon'Tor pulled her close and stroked her hair.

After a moment, Tehya pulled back to look
at him.

"You were so cross with me. Oh'Dar said it was
because you were afraid for me—but why? And I
have never heard you talk to anyone the way you
threatened the guards."

Khon'Tor said, "Oh'Dar is right. I was abrupt

because I did not trust the situation. I needed you to leave right then because I had to focus on what was happening, and I could not, thinking you might be in danger. In such instances, I am more than your mate; I am the People's Leader, including yours, and you must not question me when I give you an order."

Tehya slowly nodded. "Who were those people, Adoeete? Oh'Dar said the giant was a Sarnonn?"

"Yes. I am having difficulty accepting it myself. All of it."

"The Sarnonn were said to be Sasquatch," she said.

"We are all Sasquatch, Tehya; the People are just a different kind. And the other two with him, one was my first mate Hakani whom we all believed died long ago. And the other is a young male—I believe him to be my son. Wherever they have been living all these years, I can only surmise it is with the Sarnonn. From what he said, it seems that he considers Hakani and the young male to be his family."

Tehya lay back down next to Khon'Tor.

"Your son?"

"Hakani claimed she was seeded when she died —when we *believed* she had died."

Tehya was quiet for a moment. "Your first mate is alive. And here at Kthama—what does that mean—"

"It means *nothing other than that she did not die as we believed.* You are still my mate. You are still Third Rank. She may have returned to Kthama, but I assure you it is only temporary, and she has no place here anymore. And never will."

Tehya buried her face in his warm chest hair for a moment, inhaling his familiar, comforting scent.

"Do I now have to stay here?"

"I will not take a chance with your safety. In the past, there were problems between Hakani and me; I know you know that. Regardless of what she is here for, why she has returned, and what her intentions are, I will not trust her *or* the Sarnonn around you. Stay where I will know you are safe. There is only one way in and out of here, and there are guards stationed outside. I cannot keep track of you and them at the same time. Do you understand?"

Tehya nodded that she did. She was exhausted, and in a few moments, she was fast asleep again.

Khon'Tor remained awake for a long time. None of the scenarios that ran through his head were to his benefit.

Oh'Dar left Khon'Tor's quarters and went directly to Adia's. He entered to find her and Nadiwani administering to the sick male.

He stood over the barely moving figure and stared. The muscular structure, the body hair coloring, the shape of his extremities, angles of his face. Other than a slightly less mature build, Oh'Dar was looking at a nearly perfect copy of Khon'Tor. Even down to the silver streak running through his crown.

"How is he?" asked Oh'Dar.

"He is very sick. He has quite a fever, for one thing," explained Nadiwani. I did not find anything broken, and I suspect the only reason they were supporting him was his state of exhaustion, most likely brought on by the sickness.

"Mama. Who is he? He looks exactly like Khon'Tor."

Adia sighed. "That is because he is Khon'Tor's son."

"He is a 'Tor? He is Khon'Tor's offspring?"

"There is no question of it. You can see for yourself. Other than Akar'Tor's slightly less muscular build, it would be hard to tell them apart."

"But he is grown; where has he been all this time?" asked Oh'Dar.

"The third figure was Khon'Tor's first mate, Hakani. Yes, Hakani. She did not die, as we all believed. And she claimed to be seeded before she stepped off the path. They have been living with the Sarnonn all this time."

Oh'Dar returned his thoughts to the figure lying in front of him. He turned Akar'Tor's head from side to side, noticing swellings below the young male's ears.

"I think I know what this is," he sighed. "I had this myself not long ago. If it is the same as what I had, it will pass in two to three weeks. If it *is* what I think it is, there is no cure other than to let it work its way out.

"This swelling on the sides of his face—if the swelling transfers to other parts of his body, it can leave him unable to sire offspring. Fortunately, in my case, it never spread that far."

"We need to make him as comfortable as possible," said Adia. "We will move him elsewhere in the morning, but for tonight he can stay here so I can watch him."

"I will stay here with you, Mama, in case you need me. If you want, I can go quickly and tell Father what is happening and that we will need help in the morning to move him into another room."

Nadiwani nodded, and Adia smiled gratefully at her son.

Acaraho was just finishing up checking the placement of the extra guards. The High Protector had ordered males positioned down the corridor off which Hakani and Haan were staying. He also put a few more along the approach to Khon'Tor's quarters. He and Awan were in the process of assigning guards to posts in front of Nadiwani's quarters, the Healer's Quarters, and Oh'Dar's workshop when Oh'Dar found him. As an extraordinary precaution, Acaraho had ordered that all the guards be armed with spears.

"I came to give you an update on Khon'Tor's son. He is very ill, and Mama wants him moved to another area tomorrow if you would help or send someone else. I am going to stay with her in the Healer's Quarters tonight, in case she needs me," Oh'Dar told Acaraho.

"Thank you, son. That will be a big help. How is Tehya?"

"Khon'Tor is with her now. She was upset because she did not understand why he was so curt with her." Then Oh'Dar changed track. "Father, I have seen the sickness that the young male has. I am going to stop by the workshop and get some furs to keep him warm. We must break his fever."

Acaraho nodded. "We do not know what is going on other than that she called him Akar'Tor. And the Sarnonn's name is Haan if that helps any. They came to Kthama for help. Go back and get settled. All we have tonight is questions; hopefully, we will get some answers tomorrow," said his father.

Acaraho was up earlier than almost everyone else and was again talking to Awan about Hakani and the Sarnonn.

"They have not stirred yet this morning, Commander," reported Awan.

"They must stay in their quarters until Khon'Tor can speak with the People. I will go to them and see if they are awake now, and I want their assurance that they will stay put until I give them permission to move about."

"With all due respect, Commander, if the Sarnonn does not want to stay put—"

"I understand, Awan. But our history says they are not naturally aggressive any more than we are. And he was reasonable last night, only asking for help for his family. The guards are more a test of his intentions than an expectation that we can keep him contained. If he does not respect our authority here, that will speak volumes about their goodwill—or lack of it. And his name is Haan; we should start referring to him as such. It is impersonal to continue to call him *the Sarnonn*."

"His family? He referred to Hakani and the— This is difficult to talk about, Commander."

"You can say it, Awan. Yes, I also believe that to be Khon'Tor's son. There is no mistaking the resemblance. You remember, Hakani claimed she had been seeded by Khon'Tor before she died—"

Most of the community knew that Hakani had stepped off the edge of her own choice. But no other details had been revealed, and only he, Khon'Tor, Adia, and Awan knew the full chain of events— including Hakani's claim to be carrying Khon'Tor's offspring.

"It appears she was telling the truth. Khon'Tor and I will have to speak with them today, and I want you to join us. Someone other than I must know what is going on at present. Khon'Tor has distractions beyond the fact that Hakani is still alive."

Awan nodded.

"Have word sent to me when Khon'Tor is about. We need to deal with this as early as possible today. I already took care of some of them, but make sure *all* guards are armed with spears."

"Commander?"

"I know it has never been done. But we have to take precautions in case everything we believe about the Sarnonn, and why this one is here, turns out to be wrong. We will be drilling the guards later today. Ask Mapiya to ready the toolmakers to make more points and shafts if needed."

Acaraho slapped his First Guard on the shoulder, and Awan nodded before leaving to take care of the High Protector's orders.

Haan and Hakani were stirring in their quarters. As enormous as Haan was, Hakani had noticed that he was not encumbered by the size of the room. Nor had he had any problem walking through the corridors. For the first time, Hakani thought about the scale of Kthama.

Haan was picking at the food Acaraho had sent the night before. "How is Akar'Tor? Have you heard anything?" he asked Hakani.

'I am sorry; I know this is difficult. I know you did not want to reveal yourself to them," she replied.

Haan sighed and pushed the food around with his finger. Hakani sat on one of the seating boulders next to the table. Few of them looked large enough to support Haan's weight, so he was standing.

"When will we know if he will be alright," Haan asked again.

Hakani knew the situation was very foreign to him. And it touched her that he cared about Akar so, but then he had helped raise her son. She knew that Haan thought of Akar as his own, though they were so very different.

Haan placed his giant hand lightly on Hakani's shoulder, covering most of her back as well. "How are you feeling. Are you alright?" he asked.

"I am just tired. And I am worried, like you, and as you know, I also do not want to be here. I am doing this for Akar's sake, and I will hold my tongue around them."

"The Leader. No one will doubt he seeded Akar'-Tor." Haan made a motion indicating both the similar build and the unmistakable shock of silver hair that Akar'Tor shared with Khon'Tor.

"Yes. I hope someone will come by soon and give us an update on him. Until then, let us try to eat," she replied.

Haan nodded and went back to the food.

Hakani had no appetite. *I thought I could handle coming back to Kthama, but I did not expect to see Khon'-*

Tor. Why is he still the Leader of High Rocks? Why was he not removed in disgrace? Is it possible no one knows what he did? Surely crimes of that nature would not be dismissed—not even for the mighty Khon'Tor?

Oh'Dar rose to check on Akar'Tor. He rearranged the furs over him to keep his temperature up so the fever would break.

Adia watched him from her sleeping mat, having woken when he stirred. She noted how confident Oh'Dar was, and that he moved like a Healer. *A few nights ago, we stayed up almost until dawn as he told us about where he has been these past years. But I know there is a great deal more to learn about his experiences and where this knowledge of healing comes from.*

Knowing that Oh'Dar was tending to Akar'Tor, she lay back for a moment. *Hakani is alive. And she has returned to Kthama. Akar'Tor is clearly Khon'Tor's son. She was not lying after all about being seeded. Somehow she survived and has been living with the Sarnonn all this time? And we had no idea that there were any of them still left, at least not in our area.*

Between Oh'Dar and Hakani, she had too many questions and not enough answers.

Adia rose and checked on Akar'Tor herself. Turning to Oh'Dar, she said, "You seem to know what you are doing; I do not remember you being so confident."

"I have learned a lot, Mama. For one thing, I have found my calling—I am going to be a Healer like you."

Adia raised her eyebrows. There were no male Healers among the People. Apparently, there were with the Waschini. *Does that mean he intends to return to them?*

"Tell me what you think of Akar's condition this morning," she said, pushing that troubling thought from her mind.

"He still has a fever—high, but not life-threatening."

"When do you think we will know if he is going to be alright?"

"Not knowing when it started, I cannot answer that. We will need to ask—his mother. I do not mean to create panic, but if this is the same sickness that the Waschini get, we must consider the possibility that this is contagious," he added.

"That thought had also occurred to me." Adia's thoughts went back to when she rescued Oh'Dar. After she had brought him back, she had noticed how quiet he was, and a frightening thought had sent a bolt of fear through her soul. *I remember worrying that he might be sick and that I had brought a contagion here to High Rocks. How ironic if it turns out that it was not my offspring who would put the People at risk, but Khon'Tor and Hakani's.*

"Nadiwani will be up soon. When she comes, we can all go and find Acaraho and Khon'Tor. I think you should be there too. Akar'Tor will be fine left unattended for a brief period."

Oh'Dar nodded and rearranged Akar'Tor's covers.

Before long, Khon'Tor, Adia, Acaraho, Nadiwani, Awan, and Oh'Dar were sitting in Khon'Tor's meeting room. As they waited for Khon'Tor to start, Acaraho noted that Tehya was not among them.

"Now that we have all, hopefully, had some rest, it is time to get answers. I will make this brief as I know you all have other issues to attend. I will speak with Hakani and Haan—or at least with Hakani. I expect some of you have pressing questions of your own, though I do not want it to turn into an inquisition," Khon Tor began.

"We all have questions from different perspectives. It is possible yours are of a more personal nature, Khon'Tor; do you not wish to speak with her in private first?" asked Acaraho.

"No. I have had my fill of secrets. Whatever else there is to know, you may as well hear it when I do. The more eyes and ears, the better. I have my own distractions about the situation. I am counting on you to catch what I may miss."

Acaraho again noted that this was not the old Khon'Tor. The old Khon'Tor would never have admitted to any weaknesses nor solicited the help of others—especially not Adia. The High Protector still had strong doubts as to whether the transformation was permanent, however.

"Do you wish me to leave, Khon'Tor?" asked Oh'Dar, not sure of his place.

"No, you have been very helpful in all of this. I do not believe you are here by accident," he replied.

Adia was again pleasantly surprised by Khon'-Tor's new attitude toward Oh'Dar.

"Unless the rest of you feel very strongly about coming, Acaraho, Adia, and Oh'Dar come with me."

"I will go back and stay with Akar'Tor," Nadi-wani volunteered. "He was resting comfortably when we left him this morning. But you should know, we must consider this is not an isolated case, and there is a chance that what he has is contagious."

Under his breath, Khon'Tor let an expletive escape, *Rok Quat!* He shook his head. "Very well. Let us move." He stood, and the others followed.

Hakani called out permission for them to come in. The four of them entered in single file. Considering the size difference, and being unarmed, even with their greater numbers, Khon'Tor knew that the balance would be in Haan's favor. But the Sarnonn had shown no signs of aggression, and there was no benefit to bringing guards in as if they were on the offense.

Haan turned to greet them, taking the lead. "How is my son?"

Khon'Tor studied the behemoth Sasquatch, who was standing perfectly still, arms to his sides. His hands were twice as large as Khon'Tor's own. His thick muscular trunk sat atop equally developed thighs. His calves were well-defined, no doubt like their own, from climbing the elevations of the area. His dark body covering was thick, almost shiny in places. It was multi-colored with the hint of a greenish undertone. His dark eyes indicated intelligence and bore no animosity that Khon'Tor could see. As tall as he was, Haan did not have to stoop thanks to the height of Kthama's ceilings, even in the smaller rooms.

Adia signed back, "He is the same, no worse. We are doing all we can. It takes time." Haan nodded and looked for a place to sit. Finding nothing that would support his weight, he sat on the floor. Even seated, his size was unnerving.

Khon'Tor turned to Haan, this time speaking out loud, "Do you understand me at all?" It was possible that their root language might contain enough similarity for them to get by, as did their Handspeak.

Haan squinted as if he was partially understanding. Hakani said nothing.

Khon'Tor sighed. *This is going to take forever. I will have to ask her directly. If he cannot keep up, he will have to find out later from Hakani what we said.*

Khon'Tor abandoned Handspeak to address Hakani. "We assumed you died."

Hakani turned to Haan and translated before turning back to answer Khon'Tor.

"Though I did want to kill myself, when I stepped over the edge, I regretted it at once. I remember hitting the water, and I did not lose consciousness; somehow, I hit it just right. When I came back up, I found a log and grabbed on, and the current carried me downstream. It was very cold, and shortly afterward, I heard a terrible screamcall roar and echo down the river.

"I did my best to stay conscious, but I did not expect to live. Haan found me and took me to his community."

Khon'Tor realized that the screamcall she heard must have been Acaraho's, just as the High Protector was about to kill him.

"How far did you float downstream?"

"I do not know. I was focused on hanging on to the log. But if you are wondering why you did not know there was a Sarnonn community within our territory, they are better than we are at staying concealed. Imagine my surprise when I woke up properly, alive, staring up at their faces. I was very frightened at first. I did immediately think that they were Sarnonn, but we have thought for generations that they were extinct, or their numbers reduced to nearly zero. I soon found they meant no harm. Haan took me under his protection and ordered care for me. I could not believe I did not lose the offspring. I had nowhere to go, so I stayed. We have been there up until now. Haan raised Akar'Tor as his own. You must know that I would never have come here had your scout not come by and had Akar'Tor not been so sick. Haan would never have agreed if he did not care for Akar'Tor as his own offspring. I knew if anyone could help him, it would be Adia."

Adia and Acaraho exchanged glances at the unexpected compliment. "How long has Akar'Tor been ill?" she asked.

"Almost a month."

Oh'Dar looked at Adia and gave the smallest shake of his head. Adia did not acknowledge what she knew to be Oh'Dar's concern about how long Akar'Tor had already been ill, lest it worry Hakani.

Hakani continued, "Others in our community also had it, but Akar'Tor seemed not to be recovering. When I heard your sentries were in the area, being afraid for him, I asked Haan if we could take advantage of the opportunity to follow them here and ask for help. I did not know the way back to Kthama. He is my son," she added.

Khon'Tor took a deep breath before continuing. The Healers were right; *if it traveled through their community, whatever they have brought here must be contagious. Where do we go from here?*

"What are your intentions, Hakani? After the offspring is well," Khon'Tor said. *Assuming he does recover.* Khon'Tor had understood the look that had passed between Adia and Oh'Dar to mean the sickness was more serious than they had hoped.

The Leader waited for her answer. *Hakani knows we are compelled by our First Laws to protect, heal, and shelter anyone in need. The same laws for which she criticized Adia when she saved the Waschini offspring. The same Waschini who is now the adult caring for her son. How oddly the circle of life comes back around—I wonder if she sees the irony.*

"I mean you no harm, Khon'Tor. Though my life has not been easy the past years, it has been without altercation. I stayed with the Sarnonn because I had nowhere else to go. I did not know how to find my way back to Kthama, and besides, there was nothing left for me here but bad memories and a lifetime of festering animosity. And I expected you would have been removed from the leadership in disgrace after—"

Hakani stopped talking and closed her eyes before resuming. "We are not asking for asylum; I intend to return to Haan's people with my son."

"Very well. You and Haan will stay in these rooms unless you are taken to visit Akar'Tor and until I can address the community. They will need time to process this just as I did."

Then Khon'Tor turned to Haan and signed, "I had many questions for Hakani. I am sure she will explain them to you."

Khon'Tor looked to the others, who shook their heads. He headed for the door, and they followed him out. Once they were far down the corridor, they turned to talk.

"There is more to her story, Khon'Tor," said Acaraho.

"I know. But whether it is a matter of privacy or a matter of ill intent, I cannot tell. What do you sense, Adia?"

"At the moment, I do not feel ill intent on her part, though I do feel a struggle going on within her, which is understandable. But it is difficult for me to be completely sure when there are personal feelings involved." Adia was referring to the murkiness of her seventh sense, given the tumultuous history between Hakani and herself.

"What are the chances the male will recover? She said he had already been ill for four weeks?"

Oh'Dar answered, "I am certain that I had this same illness some time ago, Khon'Tor. Four weeks is a little longer than expected, but my experience is with the Waschini. And we do not know that her estimation is correct, so at present, I see no real cause for worry. The big problem is that from what Hakani just told us, we can be fairly certain it is contagious among the Sasquatch. Though we do not know for how long it is contagious, we have to assume that those of us who have been in close proximity to Akar'Tor have been exposed."

Khon'Tor noted the confidence with which Oh'Dar spoke. *Wherever he has been all this time and whatever he has been through have matured him considerably.*

"It would be wise to restrict contact with all of them and their movement within the community, while Akar'Tor is still sick—just in case," offered Acaraho.

"Very well," decided Khon'Tor. "At this point, it cannot be helped. For the time being, keep all the guards in place. I will call the assembly and explain the situation. Until then, I will be in my quarters. That is all."

After Khon'Tor left, Acaraho turned to the others.

"Aspects of the old Khon'Tor are returning," said Adia.

"Yes, but his actions are warranted. He is the Leader in a potentially dangerous and volatile situation. As well as his concern for his people, he also has concerns for Tehya," answered Acaraho. "The old Khon'Tor would never have worried about any one individual but himself."

Adia nodded, then changed the subject, "If this is the same sickness you had, Oh'Dar, then it means it can cross between the Waschini and the People. Hakani said that others in their community have also been ill. What else do you know about it?"

"Only what I have already told you, Mama. That in males, if it becomes severe and passes to the reproductive parts of the body, it can cause infertility," he added.

"If that is all for now, I will check in with Nadiwani," and Oh'Dar left the group. Awan joined him, leaving Acaraho and Adia alone.

"Infertility? On top of what the High Council told us we are facing?" asked Acaraho.

"Unfortunately, it would be some time before we would know if any particular male was affected. All we can do is watch for how serious it becomes and keep track. I agree, it only adds to our problems," said Adia.

She moved into the comfort of his arms for a moment before they parted.

The Call to Assembly Horn had blown, and Khon'Tor and the others waited for the room to fill. Tehya was seated with Adia and Nootau, and Acaraho stood in his usual spot, observing the crowd.

At last, Khon'Tor walked to the front of the room, raising his hand to get their attention. He carried his Leader's staff, a sobering sign of the importance of his announcement.

"The First Laws require us to help those in need —the infirm, the helpless, the sick. It was the First Laws which bound Adia to bring Oh'Dar to us all those years ago. But, even if it were not for the First Laws, Adia would have saved him anyway—such is the Healer's heart. And, I believe, the heart of all the People."

Khon'Tor paused and stepped a few feet to the side before continuing.

"Yesterday, we had to cut short our celebration of Oh'Dar's return because three visitors came to Kthama seeking our help. One of them, a young male, is with Nadiwani at present, receiving care. The other two are in their quarters, awaiting word of his status. As soon as he recovers, I expect them to return to their own community; however, in the meantime, you will need to adjust to their presence among us."

"One of them is a Sarnonn male named Haan."

Agitated chatter rolled through the crowd at the mention of a Sarnonn among them. Khon'Tor waited for it to die down, suspecting that the reaction was nothing compared to what it was about to become.

"It is important that you remember that all of us, all Sasquatch, are not aggressive. For everyone here, this is the first Sarnonn we have ever seen. As you know, we were not even sure they still existed. For centuries there have only been rumors of them. But it seems that they do exist and you will no doubt find it disturbing to be in the presence of one. But do not let Haan's physical appearance frighten you. He has done nothing but ask for help for his family.

"I do not know how long they will be staying. For the time being, they are required for the most part to remain in the quarters to which they have been assigned, but I call on you to extend them your hospitality and goodwill in the unlikely case that your paths cross. Now comes the greater challenge. Many of you will remember my first mate, Hakani. All this time we believed that Hakani had perished from her fall into the Great River—"

He paused, looking at Tehya before dragging his eyes away from her. "But we were wrong. Hakani survived and with her survived the offspring she carried. Hakani was seeded with my offspring when she attempted to take her own life. He is the one who now lies recovering in the Healer's Quarters under the care of Adia and Nadiwani."

It was not pandemonium, but it was close. Khon'Tor waited a few moments then raised his hand again for silence. When they did not comply, he slammed his Leader's staff into the stone floor. The ear-piercing crack brought everyone back to order.

"Hakani is not asking to return to Kthama. Once her son is well, she will return to Haan's community, where she has lived since we believed her to be dead. Make no mistake; Hakani has no official status in our community or as my mate. Any talk along those lines will be met with immediate consequences. Tehya is my mate, Third Rank, and I expect you to treat her as such without hesitation. I will deal directly with anyone who has a problem with that."

Technically, without the Bak'tah-Awhidi, Hakani probably *was* still his mate and *was* still Third Rank.

But Khon'Tor hoped Tehya would not realize this and would be reassured by his statement.

Tehya was watching Khon'Tor's every move. Gratitude welled in her heart at his acknowledgment of her status as his mate—his only mate.

Under the table, Adia reached over and squeezed Tehya's hand. Across the table, Oh'Dar gave her a wink and a smile.

Khon'Tor asked if there were any questions.

Mapiya stood up, "Khon'Tor, why did Hakani not return to Kthama? Are you saying she lived with the Sarnonn all these years?"

It was a fair question.

"Yes, Mapiya, she has lived with the Sarnonn since shortly after the time we believed she had died. It is no secret that the relationship between Hakani and me was strained during most of our time together. She perhaps did not want her son—our son —raised within such a destructive relationship as ours had become. There was nothing here for her to return to but more of the same struggle. From what I understand, the Sarnonn male raised the offspring as his own."

Heads turned as they looked at one another.

Khon'Tor was tired of secrets; he was prepared to offer full disclosure. *Almost.*

Someone called out, "Has she met Tehya yet?"

"Tehya was in the Great Entrance when Hakani, Haan, and the young male arrived. They have not had an opportunity to speak directly. I see no benefit in any exchange between them; therefore, I have no intention for them to interact under any circumstances."

Over my dead body is that ever going to happen, he thought, but did not say out loud. *Or better yet, over Hakani's dead body.*

Khon'Tor waited.

"Since there are no more questions, please show discretion if, at some point, they are allowed to move within our community. Hakani's life has moved on, as has my own. Even though she did not die, our relationship did—years before she attempted to take her own life. Respect that and leave the past buried where it belongs. That is all." For effect, he pounded the Leader's staff into the floor again before he stepped off the platform.

I have made it as clear as I can that they must let things be. It worries me that someone—Kahrok was it?— asked if Hakani had met Tehya. Once incited, once stirred, an appetite for drama is difficult to quench.

Khon'Tor collected Tehya on the way out, taking her hand and leading her away.

Once out of the room, he turned to her, "I do not intend to make you a prisoner in our quarters. If you wish to stay here, you may. But I do insist that wherever you go, at least one of the guards must be with you."

Tehya nodded. "I would like to visit with Adia and Oh'Dar if you do not mind. At least for a little while?"

Khon'Tor nodded and escorted her back to their table.

"Acaraho, Tehya would like to stay awhile."

To everyone's surprise, after Tehya was seated, Khon'Tor joined them, straddling the bench so that Tehya's back was to him, and she was embraced between his thighs. He wrapped his arms around her and rested them on her knees, and she leaned back against him. It was an unprecedented public display of affection from Khon'Tor and was no doubt meant to reassure Tehya.

"Khon'Tor, this illness that Akar'Tor has; you heard Hakani say that others in Haan's community had it as well. I am concerned now about it spreading among us," said Adia.

"They have already walked through the community, and several of us, including the guards who escorted Akar'Tor, have had direct contact with them as well," inserted Oh'Dar.

Acaraho said, "We will still try to minimize further spread. But then we should also prepare for an outbreak. We are fortunate the harvest was plentiful. I will ask Mapiya to spread the word for everyone to make sure the water baskets in their quarters are full, and for the kitchen areas to be well-stocked. We would be wise to assume it will spread, rather than to assume it will not."

"Can offspring also catch this, Oh'Dar?"

Adia noticed that Khon'Tor was now directing his

questions to Oh'Dar instead of her. Her maternal pride swelled.

"Yes, but it is not as serious as in adults. And females do not seem to run the risk of infertility the way males do. Of course, I am speaking about how it affects the Waschini."

"After we are done here, I will stop rotation of the out-stationed watchers to avoid bringing them in and risking their becoming infected as well. In the mean-time, I suggest we limit interaction with Hakani, Haan, and Akar'Tor as much as possible. We have all already been exposed, but there is no sense in making it worse," added Acaraho.

Khon'Tor was doing his best to hide his thoughts. *Infertility.* He looked down at his beautiful mate Tehya, leaning against him; his hopes of her producing the required heir to his leadership were now at risk.

Across the table sat Nootau, his son by Adia; the son he could not claim. Down the tunnels lay Akar'-Tor, his son by Hakani. If he could not produce an offspring with Tehya, that meant Akar'Tor was his rightful heir, a male who had been raised by the Sarnonn and had no experience of the People's ways or culture. *Impossible choices.*

As if reading Khon'Tor's mind, Acaraho volun-teered, "Why not spend time in your quarters with Tehya until this passes. You are still newly paired. I am sure you can use the time to—further your rela-tionship."

Khon'Tor nodded. He did not want to withdraw his presence from the Community. But if his fears came to pass, many of them might well be sick within a couple of weeks, and his visibility would make no difference at that point.

Tehya turned and placed her hand on Khon'Tor's chest and burrowed her fingers around in little circles. She smiled. "I am sure we can find something to do," she whispered to him, attempting to lighten his mood. Khon'Tor placed a hand over hers and gave the ghost of a smile.

Oh'Dar spoke up, "Not meaning to be indelicate, but may I suggest that it might be wise for every paired couple to spend some time together? While there is still time—"

Everyone understood what he was saying. If there was a chance of the males becoming infertile, however many might be affected, the window was still open for them to sire offspring.

"I am not sure how to send that message without frightening everyone, Khon'Tor," added Acaraho.

"Frightening or not, it could be our reality," stated the Leader. "Acaraho, re-convene the assembly this evening."

Khon'Tor suddenly realized the unprecedented way in which he and Tehya were seated and abruptly stood up to leave. Tehya rose and went with him.

Back in the Leader's Quarters, Tehya lay in Khon'-Tors arms, relaxed from their lovemating. She knew she had pleased him but that he had been distracted at the same time.

"You are worried," she said. He looked down at her, curled up against him, and nodded.

"What can I do to help?"

"Everything I have said. Stay away from Hakani and the others. Let the guards do their job. Follow my orders."

"I always follow your orders, Adoeete," she teased.

"You are improving," he said and looked off in the distance.

"So is this your new obligation now Khon'Tor?" she asked as she propped herself up on one elbow, trying to tease him out of his sullen mood. "To bed me at every opportunity so that I might produce a multitude of offspring for you?"

"I do not need an obligation to bed you. Just being around you is reason enough," and he nuzzled her neck, trying to push his worries to the back of his mind.

Was this the start of the Wrak-Ayya, the Age of Shadows? *All along, I believed it was the Waschini we should be worried about, only to have a worse threat revealed by the Council—the dwindling safe pairing combinations within our population. And now this, the possibility of infertility in our males? Perhaps this is not the Wrak-Ayya. Perhaps it is the beginning of a return to the Wrak-Wavara—the Age of Darkness.*

If we cannot mate with the Brothers, then that leaves only the Waschini—and they must never know we exist. Also, we do not want to mix our blood with theirs. All the stories of their cruelty cannot be wrong, despite the example of Oh'Dar.

Once again, Khon'Tor stood before the assembly. This time he had solicited the help of Oh'Dar in addressing the crowd. The Leader raised his hand to gather their attention.

"This morning, I told you about the visitors from the Sarnonn tribe and the reason for their coming to us. I explained about the sickness that the offspring, Akar'Tor, has. At present, he is recovering. However, he is not yet out of the woods. The illness he has can spread across our community. I am making you aware of this for several reasons. The first is that you should stay out of common areas as much as possible over the next month or so. Mapiya has already spread the word for you to keep your larders and water supplies full. If you have not taken care of that already, please do so following this meeting. Secondly, there is a particular element of risk to the males of our population, which I will ask Oh'Dar to explain before I continue."

Khon'Tor stepped back, and Oh'Dar stepped forward.

"I am sure you have heard talk about what became of me once I left Kthama. All the time I have been gone has been spent living with the Waschini. I have more to share with you about it at some point if you are interested, but while I was there, I contracted what I am confident is the same illness that Akar'Tor has. It should run its course over several weeks; however, during that period, it can be passed on to others. It does not present much threat to offspring, but it can cause complications in adults—particularly males. If you contract the illness, you will experience the usual symptoms of not feeling well—fever, chills, exhaustion, with a swelling below your ears. If the swelling extends to personal parts of the body, it can cause infertility in males. Not always, but it is a possibility. If you come down with symptoms, you must come to one of us for help. In the meantime, please stop on your way out and collect the Echinacea that my mother and I have prepared for you. It may help you ward off the illness."

Oh'Dar stepped back, and Khon'Tor took over again.

"I do not wish to alarm you, but I want to stress to you the challenges we may be facing. Therefore, I am asking all of you who are paired to—increase your mating activities. Should the worst happen and a number of us end up unable to sire offspring, it would behoove us as a community to have as many of our females seeded as possible."

Seeing the pinched faces in the crowd, Khon'Tor smiled, "I trust that of all the directives I have given you in the past, you will find this one the most pleasurable with which to comply." A roll of quiet laughter rippled across the crowd.

"That is all," and he stepped down from the platform just in time to meet up with Nadiwani.

"Khon'Tor, there has been a development."

Now what?"

Akar'Tor is awake. And he is asking for his parents."

CHAPTER 5

Khon'Tor sent word for the guards outside Hakani and Haan's living quarters to escort them to the care area to see Akar'-Tor. As much as he did not want any more exposure to the sickness, he could not let them visit without an authority present.

Hakani and Haan entered the care area and found Akar'Tor lying awake, just as they had been told. Khon'Tor stood with one of the guards as far to the back as he could.

Nadiwani explained to the visitors that Akar'Tor was still weak, and they could not stay long.

Haan crouched down so he would not loom over Akar'Tor, while Hakani took her offspring's hand. The young male lifted his head and signed, "Where am I, Mama?"

Hakani replied, "You are safe and getting the care you need. You must rest. Are you hungry?"

Akar'Tor was not and drifted back to sleep, exhausted. He did not seem to have noticed Khon'Tor.

While he had the two there, Khon'Tor took advantage of the opportunity to ask them some more questions. "Hakani, as you can see, he is improving. But he will need to stay until he fully regains his strength. Unless, of course, you would prefer to take him back and care for him yourselves?"

"Perhaps in a few days, Khon'Tor. But yes, to remain here for now would probably be easier on him."

Haan was frowning, struggling to follow the conversation—but Khon'Tor would not accommodate him, considering the severity of the situation.

"How many of the others in your community are sick?" he asked.

"Right now, perhaps half. Haan had it some time ago but recovered, as did I. I suspect we passed it to Akar'Tor ourselves. If we had not recovered, we would not have been able to come here," she explained.

Why did you come here? What is the rest of the story Hakani? I know you are not telling me everything. Do you even recognize when you are lying? Khon'Tor's familiar old anger with her was rising.

Nadiwani stepped forward to join the discussion, "Do you have any idea where it came from? Has anyone from your group been in contact with any other group recently?"

"No. We keep to ourselves, just as the People do. I am sorry I cannot be of more help. We had the same questions," offered Hakani.

"Let us give them some privacy for a few moments," and Nadiwani led Khon'Tor out into the corridor.

"I heard what Hakani said, Khon'Tor, but in my estimation, she still does not look well herself, and I wonder if the illness can relapse. She has not taken those wraps off since she arrived. I realize that the home of the full-coated Sarnonn was probably a colder environment for her, but by now, she should have discarded them. Perhaps she has a fever and is chilled. And there is certainly more that she is not telling us. "

"We are all thinking that, Nadiwani. Unfortunately, only time will tell. All we can do now is to take precautions and try to contain the spread of the illness. It is what it is at this point."

They waited for Hakani and Haan to exit, and Khon'Tor left while the guards returned them to their quarters. Nadiwani went back in to Akar'Tor.

Old feelings were being resurrected in Khon'Tor —feelings he did not want brought back to life again. Intense, angry, resentful, *aggressive* feelings that he had believed dead with Hakani.

It was not as bad as Khon'Tor had feared. It was worse. Within several weeks, nearly a quarter of the community was ill. Sleeping mats were lined up wall to wall along the hallways—to the point that there was no more room, so the sick were being nursed in their own quarters by their families where ever possible. Those who did not live in committed family pods administered to those who shared their gender groups. Once the first round started to recover, another group came down with it.

The older females who could worked tirelessly to make new sleeping mats. As people recovered, the old mats were dragged out and burned. Wrappings were washed and dried over the fires. There was a constant procession of fresh water being brought in, used, and taken away. Those who were not involved in helping Adia and the others were busy trying to keep everyone fed and clean. The males gathered firewood, while offspring collected leaves, grasses, and other bedding material for the sleeping mats.

Adia tried to spend as much time as possible with Akar'Tor, knowing he had to be uncomfortable at Kthama. She felt he appreciated her tending to him. But she and Nadiwani were quickly becoming exhausted. As much as she did not want to expose the Brothers, Adia needed help. She asked Khon'Tor for permission to send for Honovi, provided the risks were explained to her as well as to Chief Ogima Adoeete and Is'Taqa. She wanted it made very clear that Honovi was under no obligation to come.

Acaraho himself traveled to meet with the Brothers' Chiefs to share the news of their situation and make a request for assistance.

Standing just inside the tree line, out of sight of the rest of the village and a good distance from where the Chiefs were standing, he thanked them both for coming.

"What has happened, High Protector?" asked Is'Taqa. Acaraho's daylight visit gave great cause for concern.

"Visitors have come to Kthama. But not just any visitor. Hakani, Khon'Tor's first mate whom we believed to have died, has returned, bringing Khon'Tor's son with her."

The two men stared unmoving, bracing themselves as they recognized from Acaraho's body language that there was more coming. "All this time that we believed her to be dead, she has been living with a Sarnonn community."

"Sarnonn? The Ancients still walk Etera?"

"Yes, Ogima Adoeete. We are still dealing with the shock of the discovery ourselves. But there is more; the young male, who is clearly Khon'Tor's offspring, is ill. That is what caused them to reveal themselves by coming to Kthama, looking for Adia's help. But what he has is spreading through our community. It has become more than Adia and Nadiwani can handle. We would not ask if the need were not great. Knowing that what we are asking will put them at risk—" He explained the details of the sickness.

Chief Ogima raised his hand. "You wish the help of Ithua?"

"Or Honovi—whoever you can send. But they must know what they are walking into."

"We will speak with them," said Is'Taqa. Acaraho nodded, thanked them, and turned back to Kthama.

Within a few days, Honovi arrived with her eldest daughter, Acise. They came laden with more Echinacea as well as Black Elderberry and Ginger. Oh'Dar made a point of being there when they arrived, knowing that Acise would have to adjust to being around the People, just as had Honovi years ago. Oh'Dar watched as she looked around the huge Great Entrance and tried not to stare at the guards who came to take charge of their ponies.

Adia was there to greet them.

As they walked into the Great Entrance, Acise looked up at the high ceilings and glanced around the wide expanse. Lined up on the left and right were several large males armed with spears, watching their arrival.

Acise exclaimed to Honovi, "Oh, Momma."

Honovi smiled and put her arm around her daughter, "I remember my first visit here, too. You will become used to it in time. Just try to stay focused on what you are doing and do not look around too much at first if you are in a group of the People."

"Thank you for coming," said Adia. "We had great reservations about asking this of you. Oh'Dar will take you to where you will be staying, and I will be around to check on you later. If you need anything, as before, Honovi, you know you can ask anyone for help.

Oh'Dar picked up their travel satchels and took Honovi and Acise to get themselves set up in his workroom. It was a converted living quarters, so there was more than enough room for the two women to work and live there. He was so busy helping care for everyone that he caught sleep wherever he could.

Kweeuu had moved in with Nadiwani and Nootau, and the young male somehow found time to take care of the giant grey wolf.

When Oh'Dar saw Acise at the Great Entrance, his thoughts flashed back to his last night with the Brothers, when she had scooted up next to him in the night and laced her fingers between his.

Over the next few days, her presence began tormenting him more and more. He could tell she was glad to see him as she looked up at him through veiled eyes that seemed to follow him wherever he went. She was beautiful, like her mother. Long straight black hair fell over her shoulders; ample breasts sat above a small waist that curved down to meet her generous hips. He caught himself watching her walk away at every opportunity. She was also kind, funny, intelligent, and a dedicated worker.

I have to stop. I do not want to hurt Acise, but nothing can happen between us. I cannot let myself develop feelings for her; it will only make it harder to go back to Grandmother. And I have not even told Mama that I am leaving.

Oh'Dar vowed to speak with Acise at the first opportunity and gently head her off. Then he tried to force her out of his mind, which their circumstances made impossible.

In addition to being a distraction, Oh'Dar found Acise to be a considerable help. She had learned much from her mother, Honovi, as well as from Ithua, the Brothers' Medicine Woman. She and her mother worked together seamlessly, each instinctively knowing what the other would be reaching for next and having it at the ready. She did the same for him, somehow knowing what he needed before he did. He could not have asked for a better helpmate, which made the idea of rejecting her all the harder. She was easy to talk to, and he enjoyed her company.

However, he knew Acise and Honovi would be there for some time, and besides not wanting to hurt her, he did not want their time together to be stilted.

"So, you went to find your Waschini family," commented Acise as they worked together one afternoon. "We did not have much time to talk back at the Village before you left."

"Yes. As you know, my first mother and father

were killed not long after I was born. But my father's mother, my grandmother, is still alive. They were kind to me. Not what you would have thought, from what we have heard of the Waschini."

"Would you please break this one up? It is too large for me to crush," Acise asked. She handed Oh'Dar a clump of Ginseng root, allowing her hand to brush against his.

Honovi watched her eldest daughter flirting with Oh'Dar, but to his credit, he ignored the contact.

Later, Acise squeezed past him around the work table, putting her hands on his hips as she did. Again, Oh'Dar did not acknowledge her actions.

Honovi also noticed how Acise stared at Oh'Dar when he was not looking. And even though he seemed to be doing his best to ignore her flirtations, she caught how Oh'Dar's eyes lingered over her daughter. But to be fair, Acise was clearly acting the temptress.

There was a fit about it that made sense to Honovi, perhaps in part because her father had been Waschini, but she was not sure about Oh'Dar's future and was naturally protective of her daughter. After all, Honovi knew how the young man struggled over his place in the world. Even though Oh'Dar seemed more settled than he had ever been, she still sensed restlessness in him. Before, she had thought the interest was only on Acise's side. If she had noticed earlier that what was going on was between the two of them, she would have talked it over in far more detail with Is'Taqa. Now she was isolated here and could not reach her mate.

Haan stood over his adopted son as Hakani gave Akar'Tor some water.

Recovery had been slow. However, none of the extended swelling had occurred, which gave them hope that he would still be able to seed offspring. However, many in Khon'Tor's community were not so fortunate—with about a fifth of the males affected showing signs that the inflammation had spread to their reproductive organs.

Akar'Tor looked up at his father, "I am feeling better now. When can we go home?"

Haan replied, "Not yet. You are not ready to go back. We have to stay until you are fully well."

"Mama, are you alright?"

Hakani looked over at Haan before answering, "Yes, I am," and uncharacteristically, she added, "I love you, Akar."

Akar'Tor turned toward the wall and went back to sleep.

Hakani looked back at Haan, who signed, "You have not told them yet." She just shook her head. No.

Khon'Tor and Adia stood talking in one of the small rooms.

"I do not know how much longer I can stay out of Akar'Tor's sight. He is going to be moving about soon," said Khon'Tor.

"I understand, but I assume Hakani told him who sired him. I have my own concerns with Nootau. I keep picturing them side by side; I am afraid the resemblance will be unmistakable. So far, everyone still assumes that Acaraho is Nootau's father—as does he."

Khon'Tor turned to catch Adia's eye and waited for her to look up at him before continuing.

"Adia, again, I thank you for withdrawing your accusation with the High Council. And for standing in my defense. After what I did to you—"

He remembered her saying that she had lost more than her maidenhood when he violated her, that she had lost the Leader she looked up to and needed. As with everything she had said that day, the impact of that statement had stayed with him.

Adia looked up at Khon'Tor.

"What happened was a long time ago. Destroying you would have destroyed us all. And you have changed. We all see it. And despite how hard it was, something good came of it. You have a son and a daughter. As do I," she said.

"Neither of whom I can claim, as you have said in the past, for risk of destroying them and everyone else with the truth. And now, Akar'Tor. But he knows nothing of our culture. And even if he wanted to, he cannot stay. Not if it means Hakani and Haan stay as well."

"Tehya is young, and you still have time. We all like her, and she adores you. Truly, everyone is glad to see you finally have some peace and happiness."

Khon'Tor looked off in the distance. "Not everyone here, not any longer."

"Hakani may not even realize you have a new mate. Besides, she will not be staying. She said they would leave once Akar'Tor was well," Adia said.

"I am not convinced. There is something more going on."

Adia nodded. "I agree with you about that. And if that is true, it will become apparent in time. I am going to tend to Akar'Tor."

With that, Khon'Tor took his leave too and went to find Acaraho. He looked around Kthama as he walked through the hallways. *If it were not for Adia, I would not still be here. Hakani almost destroyed me, with my help. And she still could. I will not let Hakani return me to what I was. No matter what else happens to me, if I do that, she wins."*

So far, none of the Leaders had gotten sick. Adia gave credit to their dedicated intake of Echinacea and the supplemental herbs Honovi had brought. But fatigue was setting in, and with that, she knew their risk of infection increased.

The main eating area was fairly empty because so many were ill and staying in their quarters now. The females who were not ill or not nursing sick relatives did their best to prepare meals for those who needed them.

Adia and Oh'Dar sat together, both exhausted. Oh'Dar looked at his mother, who usually sat upright, now leaning her elbows on the table.

"You need to get some rest, Mama. There is only so much any of us can do," he said.

"We still have not gotten a chance to talk further about where you have been and what you experienced, Oh'Dar."

"I know; we have both been too exhausted. I promise we will as soon as this has passed. It was certainly unexpected. Is the High Council still coming?"

"Not for a few months yet. If there is not a reasonable expectation that this will have passed, we shall have to cancel the meeting. Surely it will have run its course by then. It is important that the assembly take place." She did not explain, as it was not for anyone outside the inner circle to know the matters to be discussed. The People had enough on their minds without adding the threat of eventual extinction to the list of worries.

Adia made a mental note to ask that Oh'Dar be

somehow included in the High Council meeting when it took place. If their choice as a People included inter-breeding with the Waschini in order to survive, his demeanor might help assuage the belief in the Waschini's natural destructive inclinations. She was fairly confident that most of those in attendance, along with most of the People, had never met a Waschini. The knowledge most of them had only consisted of stories and hearsay. In addition, Oh'Dar could provide first-hand experience about the Waschini's world.

Adia's eyes brightened as she said, "I notice that Acise seems to like you."

"Oh. Really?" Oh'Dar looked down. Adia chuckled.

"You are not fooling me, son. I have seen you looking at her, too. Is there something I should know?"

"She is very kind. Smart. Pretty. I have gotten to know her some from working together, and I like her very much. But I am not ready to settle down, Mama. I still do not know where I belong."

Adia's smile faded. She had hoped he had returned for good. She wanted to ask, but she was just too exhausted.

Shortly, Nootau and Nimida joined them. Adia suppressed a frown at seeing them together—again.

"We have been helping Honovi and Acise grind up Ginseng root," offered Nootau.

"Where's Kweeuu?" asked Oh'Dar.

"He is in our quarters. I do not want him

wandering around with the—with Haan here. I do not know how he might react to Kweeuu, or Kweeuu to him," Nootau explained. Oh'Dar nodded.

"We know very little about the Sarnonn," Adia thought to herself, *except that we are the result of their finding a way to mate with the Brothers.*

At about that time, Haan appeared at the entrance with Akar'Tor and Hakani. Everyone in the room turned to look. Nimida looked at Akar'Tor. Then back at Nootau. Then back at Akar'Tor, but said nothing. Adia's heart skipped a beat.

"That is Akar'Tor? He looks exactly like—"

Adia dropped her food.

"—Khon'Tor."

"Silly!" said Nootau. "Khon'Tor is Akar'Tor's father, Nimida. Do you not remember? Hakani was Khon'Tor's first mate," he said as he poked Nimida in the ribs with his elbow. Nimida rubbed her side and scowled at Nootau, her eyes twinkling.

"I should go over and see what they need," and with that, Adia picked up what was left of her food to drop off at the refuse station on her way to speak with Hakani and Haan.

"What do you need? Can I help you?" Adia asked, using Handspeak.

"Akar'Tor wanted to see Kthama," replied Hakani. "Khon'Tor gave us permission to leave our quarters briefly. We thought a short walk might do him good. But we also came to see if there was anything here that might appeal to his appetite." Then she turned to Haan and said something almost intelligible.

So they do have a verbal language, I can make out quite a bit of what she is saying. No doubt, with practice, we could learn it. I must tell Acaraho and Khon'Tor.

Adia hated pretending she did not understand most of what Hakani had said. Playing along, however, she turned to Akar'Tor and signed, "How are you feeling? You must be tired." Akar'Tor signed back, "I am much better, thank you. I am grateful for your kindnesses."

Adia smiled, realizing he must have been conscious enough to know she had tended to him a great deal of the time. She nodded, "Let me know if you need something."

As she turned to leave, out of the corner of her eye she saw Hakani start to fold.

Haan caught Hakani up just as her knees buckled, and he swept her up easily into his arms. Adia swung around to look at her, and Oh'Dar came running over. Hakani had passed out cold.

"Haan, carry Hakani carefully and come with us," and Adia led the way to The Healer's Quarters. She wanted privacy in which to examine her.

Haan laid her down on one of the mats, and Adia and Oh'Dar crouched over her. They could find no obvious reason for Hakani's collapse.

Thinking Haan might know something, Adia

looked up at him and asked, "What could be wrong with her? Do you know?"

Haan made a single sign in reply. "Offling."

Adia signed back, not recognizing the sign. "Offling?"

Haan made a gesture of cradling an offspring.

Oh'Dar and Adia looked at each other, wide-eyed. Hakani had been seeded by a Sarnonn?

CHAPTER 6

Adia's mind was racing. She knew it should be possible for the two tribes to interbreed and produce healthy offspring. According to the ancient stories, they shared a common root, the Sarnonn having crossed with the Brothers to produce the People. But for the father to be a Sarnonn and the mother to be one of the People was a dangerous combination.

So this is the rest of the story, what Hakani has been hiding from us. She knew this offspring could not go full term. She came to get help for herself as well as Akar'Tor. But why cover it up? Can she not simply tell the truth about anything?

"Oh'Dar, please find Nadiwani, Khon'Tor, and Acaraho. Oh, wait—never mind, stay here with me for now. I cannot think straight at the moment."

Hakani moaned and turned her head to the side. As she became conscious, Adia helped her sit up.

"What happened?" Hakani's hand went to her head.

"You fainted. In the eating area. We brought you here so we could take care of you privately," answered Adia.

"I am sorry. I am just tired, that is all," Hakani replied.

Adia sighed. "Hakani, Haan told us. How far along are you?" she asked.

Akar'Tor and Haan were standing along the stone wall of their quarters, watching. Hakani caught Haan's eye and motioned for him to take Akar'Tor out of the room. Once Akar'Tor had gone, she returned her attention to Adia.

Hakani left out a big sigh. "About five months," she replied, switching to verbal language.

Adia and Oh'Dar looked at each other. They had not noticed because of her bulky, heavy wraps.

"Is that why you came here? Not only for Akar'-Tor, but because you knew you were in trouble? And does Haan understand the issues of your being with his offspring?"

"Yes, I brought us here for both our sakes. But I do not know if Haan fully understands the situation. At least, he did not understand the risk at the time I became seeded."

"Is this your first seeding? By Haan, I mean?" Though he was certain the answer had to be yes, Oh'Dar had to ask.

"Yes. For almost this whole time we did not— there was someone else— But then—"

Adia interrupted her. "You do not owe us an explanation, Hakani. But we need to deal with the situation. You cannot possibly carry this offspring to term. You will never be able to deliver it. Do you understand?"

"Yes. I do not know what I was thinking; it was a weak moment. And he has been very kind to me, all these years. He saved me, cared for me. And he raised Akar'Tor. I do care for him," and she looked away.

Acaraho appeared, and Adia looked over at her mate before turning back to Hakani.

"I think you are well enough to go back to your quarters. Do you think so?"

Hakani nodded. Adia asked Acaraho to have Haan come back in and then signed to Haan to take his mate and Akar'Tor back to where they were staying. Haan scooped up Hakani and gently carried her out.

Acaraho stood waiting for someone to tell him what was going on.

"Hakani collapsed in the meal area, and I had Haan bring her here so we could check her out. Acaraho, she is seeded," explained Adia.

"By *Haan*?" Acaraho frowned, then shook the images out of his head.

"Yes, unfortunately. That is what she was not

telling us. At least, I cannot believe there could be anything else."

Acaraho made a steeple with his fingers in front of his lips, thinking.

"We have to force the offspring to be born early—but as late as possible. Too early, and it will not survive on its own. If we wait too long, then it will be too large to be born. Mother and offspring will both die——horribly," Adia continued.

"What do you need from me?"

"There is nothing you can do. Just pray that we can handle this and that the offspring will survive. We *have* to induce her labor early; there is no other way. But if the offspring does not live, who knows what Haan might do, having to deal with the death of his offspring because we induced it too early. We believe the Sarnonn are not violent, any more than we are—but still, we know very little about them. All we have are stories—just as with the Waschini.

"All these years, they have managed to stay hidden from us. Why?"

"I have had the same thoughts. But as for Haan, we cannot take the chance of his misunderstanding. Even if he does understand, it would be upsetting for him. And he could do a lot of damage, even in a short emotional outburst. We need to talk to Khon'Tor," said Acaraho.

He saw that Adia had sat down and was resting her head in her hands. "You look tired," he said.

"I am," she admitted.

He came over and took both her hands in his and squatted down to make eye contact with her.

"Take the night off. Please; we can spend the time together." Then with a twinkle, he added, "I promise to let you sleep."

Adia smiled back. "How did I get so lucky, Acaraho? Despite all our troubles, I am so truly blessed by having you." She brought one of his hands to her face and placed it against her cheek.

Oh'Dar smiled as he watched the tender display between the only parents he had ever known.

More rested the next morning, Adia decided that the leadership had to meet. Acaraho sent word, and the group assembled in Khon'Tor's meeting room.

The Leader was the last to arrive. Looking around, he asked, "Where's Oh'Dar?"

Adia blinked. "Do you want Oh'Dar here?"

"He has been helpful so far. Depending on what you want to discuss, his viewpoint may be insightful."

"Anyone else?" asked Acaraho.

Khon'Tor looked around the room. Adia, his Second Rank, Tehya who was Third Rank, and Acaraho—who had no official rank according to the Second Laws but was functionally Second in Command. In day-to-day operations, he was Khon'-

Tor's right hand, but in a state of crisis, he officially ranked directly under the Leader.

"Nadiwani—if she can be spared." Khon'Tor was trying not to create any more secrets. Those he already carried were burden enough.

Acaraho dispatched a guard who was standing outside to find Oh'Dar and the Helper.

Adia filled the time. "It has been too long since we all met. I think it is time we share our knowledge, and perhaps we can piece together what we must do next. The High Council follow-up meeting will not be that far off, for one thing."

The guard returned shortly, and Oh'Dar and Nadiwani entered, both looking confused. Nadiwani had started biting at her nails, something she had never done before but was certainly doing now.

"Sit," ordered Khon'Tor.

They sat.

"Adia called this meeting, and she was right to do so. It is your meeting, Healer," and Khon'Tor gave her the floor.

"First of all, there has been a development. It does not have to dominate this meeting because we all need to share what we know and have observed. But you should all know that Hakani is with offspring."

Khon'Tor shook his head as if he had been expecting it. Or something, at least.

"Am I to assume by Haan?" he asked, already anticipating the answer.

"Yes. I am sure you realize this, but let me make it clear. A female of the People is structurally too small to carry a Sarnonn offspring to term. Had it been the other way around, one of our males seeding a Sarnonn, there would be little risk. As it is, though, unless we force it to be born early, both the offspring and Hakani will die. There is no way the offspring can be born naturally."

"I understand this. My grandmother's stable master breeds horses," Oh'Dar volunteered.

"Is it too late to—" Nadiwani offered then stopped, not sure if the male population knew there were medicines which would cause a miscarriage if used in the first few months.

"Yes, it is too late. She is too far along. And I do not think she would, anyway. She seems to feel she owes him this. It seems complicated."

"So, all we *can* do is induce labor early." Nadiwani sighed.

"Yes, and if we do that, there is still the risk that the offspring might not survive. We do not know how Haan might react to that," Adia added, looking over at Acaraho. "That is all I have to report."

Nadiwani took a deep breath, though she was becoming more used to being the center of attention. "As far as the sickness goes, about half of those who got sick first should be coming out of it soon. The rest will recover a couple of weeks after because it seems to take about three weeks to run its course.

"I am surprised none of us has come down with it

yet. That is bad news because it means there is a chance that if and when we do, it could roll through us all at the same time. We are hoping that since Oh'Dar has already had this illness, he will be immune.

"We have been burning the bedding and replacing with new. And once this is over, we should do our best to clean or burn anything else that people have come in long contact with. Khon'Tor, I know you do not like fires, but—" It was a long speech for Nadiwani, and her voice faded away.

Khon'Tor waved his hand, "Acaraho asked me for permission at the start."

Since there was a pause, and because he was not used to sitting, Acaraho stood up and started walking around.

"As far as the watchers go, I have lost very few, most likely due to their remote locations. Of the guards, about a fourth are sick. That leaves me short-staffed either outside Kthama or inside. At present, I have retained the full complement inside. Khon'Tor, let me know if that does not meet with your approval. I have sent a few watchers back down the route we believe Haan and Hakani took. Most likely, one of our sentries unknowingly passed their shelter —or wherever they are living—and perhaps that is what flushed Hakani out. Or perhaps she had this planned all along, and it had nothing to do with our attempts to find other Sasquatch communities. But as it stands, we have no idea where, or how, they live."

Khon'Tor listened carefully, formulating a plan as they spoke. "Oh'Dar?"

Oh'Dar took a deep breath. "I told you before that, depending on where it spreads, this illness can cause sterility in males. From what I have seen, very few of our males have been affected."

"Anything else? Keep talking—anyone," the Leader directed.

"Hakani never leaves Haan's side. I do not know if that is because she is afraid he will be uncomfortable here without her, or for some other reason. I hate to be suspicious," said Adia. Then she added, "It is hard to let the past go."

"Looking at Haan's size, I find it difficult to believe that he would be uncomfortable anywhere. As one of our larger males, I can say that being the largest in the room tends to give one a sense of—confidence," Acaraho offered.

Adia added, "Immediately after she collapsed and we were tending to her, she talked to him in the Sarnonn language. It was similar to ours. I could make quite a bit of it out as they were speaking slowly. Definitely more guttural, more slurred. So, the good news is, at least we could potentially learn to communicate with them other than through Handspeak. I truly do not think it would take that long; it is more a matter of developing an ear for it."

"What do we know about our differences?" asked Khon'Tor.

"Other than the obvious; height, weight, girth, the fact that they are covered with thick hair, not much. He is slower moving, but we cannot assume that is always the case. He may be suppressing his motions so as not to frighten us. I remember that the first time I met Honovi, I instinctively did the same thing. His lack of dexterity and his basic Handspeak makes him appear—less bright than us. Again, I do not know if that is true."

Adia waited for Acaraho to finish before adding to what he had said, "That is a good point. About his Handspeak. When Hakani spoke out loud to him, she spoke quickly. It was very fluid and—complex. In other words, it was not the verbal equivalent of the stilted way they talk with Handspeak."

Everyone nodded, and then silence fell. Khon'Tor got up and walked around the perimeter of the room. He stopped in front of Acaraho.

"What is the worst that could happen if he became violent?"

"I hate to hazard a guess."

"Do so regardless, Acaraho. We are just throwing ideas around here. No one is going to hold you to it," Khon'Tor prompted him.

"I am sure you already know. The worst scenario is that if we were unprepared, he would kill and injure a number of us before someone figured out how to bring him down; he has the strength and endurance. The number of wounded would be considerable, and it is a scenario we cannot risk. On the other hand, armed with spears and with the drills that Awan and I are supervising, perhaps six or seven of us could take him out, though there would be losses on our side even at that. And as you have no doubt noticed, I *have* outfitted the guards with spears. But the Sarnonn, like us, are purportedly not aggressive or violent. Unless Hakani tells him, he will not know that the guards are not ordinarily armed, and even that could have changed during the time she was away. I find it an acceptable trade-off."

"Everything we *hear* is that they are not aggressive and of course, neither are we. But if anyone remembers Adia confronting Hakani when she hoisted Oh'Dar up over her head in front of the community, I think we can all agree that when our offspring are involved, we are all capable of fury," Khon'Tor said.

Oh'Dar looked over at his mother, eyebrows raised. Adia shook her head *no* at him and raised her palm, indicating that now was not the time to get into *that* story.

The Leader continued. "The fact is, we know very little about them. That they have lived here in our territory, undiscovered, speaks to their abilities. His hair has an undertone to it that is nearly green, almost iridescent. Perhaps that aids with camouflage; I do not know. After this has passed, we will need to concentrate on establishing solid relations between us. Assuming the situation with Hakani's seeding does not destroy any chance of that."

"Tehya, you have not said anything yet," and Khon'Tor turned to his young mate.

Tehya looked around the room and swallowed, her shyness in full force.

"I have been fairly isolated, so I do not have a lot of observations. But I would say that from what everyone has said, it would be wise for someone to try to get close to Haan. It is possible that Hakani is keeping him from connecting to us for a reason. I have heard the stories of how Hakani intentionally stepped off the edge of the path. You all seem to think she is dishonest. So we do not know it is the story she told him when he found her. If the worst happens and the offspring does not survive, it would be good for Haan to think of us as people and not just nameless targets for his anger or grief."

Then she added, "It should probably be someone who has no history with Hakani."

Khon'Tor knew she meant herself. He did not like that. He did not like that one bit.

"No. I will not allow it."

"Khon'Tor!"

Khon'Tor suspected they were about to have their first fight. *And in front of everyone. Well, I just told myself I was tired of secrets.*

"It is too dangerous."

He walked back over and sat down next to her.

"You cannot keep me isolated forever, Khon'Tor.

If I am to be part of the leadership, I have to share in the risks, too," she said softly.

"No. Next topic," Khon'Tor said, holding his palm up as he rose again.

"No. We need to talk about this now."

Khon'Tor shook his head and turned back to face her.

"Of anyone I would put near Haan, *you* would be my last choice. I understand what you are saying about not having a history with Hakani. But I *do,* and by default, it involves you as well. And I understand that you want to contribute. Perhaps I have been wrong in keeping you sequestered, but it was out of love, never out of an intention to cut you off from the group. If Hakani wanted to strike me to the core, and I am not willing to take the chance that she does not, all she would have to do is harm you. *I will not risk you, Tehya.*

Nobody stirred. Khon'Tor, Leader of the largest population of the People, had just splayed his heart open in front of everyone there.

Tehya nodded slowly. "All right. I understand. I withdraw my suggestion." She rose and went over to him. He put his arms awkwardly around her, using every bit of willpower to maintain his composure and deeply uncomfortable that others were watching their personal display.

Having a relationship I value is harder than having one I do not. In the past, I would not have bothered to console Hakani, nor did I care if she was upset. I do not like displaying this side of me. I am still the Leader of the People of the High Rocks.

The rest all looked at each other while they waited for the lovers to return their attention to the group. After a moment, Khon'Tor released Tehya and they rejoined the group together.

Acaraho was clearly disturbed. "If this is a time for speaking plainly, then let me speak."

Khon'Tor nodded for Acaraho to continue.

"As much as we all want to believe that Hakani has changed, none of us do. All of us struggle to trust her. We know that people can change," and Acaraho tried not to look in Khon'Tor's direction. "But that does not mean she has."

Khon'Tor nodded; he was still fighting old feelings of resentment against her.

Acaraho continued, "She came to us needing help for Akar'Tor, but also for herself. She did not disclose that she was seeded by Haan. Had she not fainted, I am not sure we would know yet. But what reason was there for withholding that information? It was going to come out sooner or later. Deceit for deceit's sake? We cannot assume that her hatred of you, Khon'Tor, and you, Adia, has completely vanished. And even if she made peace with it over the years, that does not mean it cannot be triggered again. She came here needing our help. Once it is given, who knows what may come thereafter."

Acaraho walked over to where Tehya was sitting.

"We know what Hakani is capable of—from her

reckless dramatics over Oh'Dar's presence, to her last act of trying to kill Nootau. She has proven there is little she will not do to strike at those she feels have wronged her. So, to your point, Tehya, and to yours, Khon'Tor, the last person we want to put around her *or* Haan would be Tehya. *Everyone* knows how happy you two are. A blind hawk in the treetops during a midnight storm could see it. As you said, if she wanted to crush you, Khon'Tor, harming Tehya would be the most effective way. We cannot take that chance."

Khon'Tor was relieved by Acaraho's statement. *And they do not know the half of the extent of what she did. They have no idea about her being with offspring by another male. But then, I am far from innocent myself, and I can only continue to pray that I may have a few years of happiness with Tehya before justice hunts me down.*

He continued, "I will not downplay my own part in the troubles between Hakani and myself. But it does not change the fact that she could have lingering animosities."

Oh'Dar went over and took the seat next to Tehya, vacated by Khon'Tor, and put one of his hands on hers.

"So how do we move forward?" asked Adia.

Khon'Tor walked back and faced the group.

"Acaraho, continue as you are, maintaining as full a complement of guards within Kthama as you can. We have never armed our indoor guards with spears, but I support your decision. We still have watchers on the Brothers' territory and a few others in their usual posts. With the Sarnonn's abilities, if they wanted to sneak up on us, they would have by now, but we still have to try. If we need someone to get close to Haan, who also has little history with Hakani, that would be Nadiwani and maybe Oh'Dar.

"As far as the rest of us and the sickness is concerned, if there is a chance it can hit all of us at once, then half of us need to stop taking the Echinacea and any other precautions. The sooner we get it over with, the better. Acaraho, you and I must decide between us. Adia, you and Nadiwani must decide between you. That leaves Oh'Dar, whom we assume is immune—and Tehya."

Tehya let out a deep sigh and closed her eyes.

"Khon'Tor, I believe I am already coming down with it. It started this morning," she said.

Khon'Tor dug his nails into his palms.

"Tehya, when we leave here, we will collect your personal belongings and then go to the Healer's Quarters. I will care for you myself," offered Adia. "Khon'Tor, with your permission, of course."

Khon'Tor nodded and dug his nails deep. Blood seeped through his fingers.

"As far as the High Council meeting goes, we may have to decide whether to cancel it or not. But we do not need to make that decision now.

"Nadiwani, continue to keep me posted about the numbers of those who are sick and those who are not. You can come to me directly or submit your report through Acaraho."

"Adia, thank you for calling this meeting. We will reconvene in four days unless there is a need to do so sooner. Everyone keep alert. More than ever, I need you all to stay focused and on task."

Khon'Tor scanned the group looking for anything left unsaid. Seeing only nodding heads, he dismissed them. "That is all."

Adia and Acaraho followed Tehya back to the Leader's Quarters. Acaraho wanted to make sure that she had the strength to walk there. They waited while she assembled some items in a small bag, and then escorted her back to the Healer's Quarters.

While they were gone, Nadiwani and Oh'Dar prepared a place for Tehya. Nadiwani placed a fresh sleeping mat for her, thankful that the older females were staying ahead of the demand. Oh'Dar went to his workshop to get a fresh wolf pelt.

Oh'Dar entered his workshop, forgetting that Honovi and Acise were using it as their home base. He breathed in deep the smell of tanned hides, sage, lavender, and wood.

"Oh'Dar!" Acise startled as he stepped into the room. Wiping her hands on a drying cloth, she came over to him.

"I am sorry, Acise. I forgot that you and your

mother were working here. I have just come to get a fresh wolf pelt for someone," he said as he stepped around her.

Just as he passed, she reached out and grabbed his arm. Oh'Dar looked around the room and realized they were alone—something he had tried to avoid.

She put her hands on his chest, moving them up toward his shoulders and looked up at him with willing eyes.

Oh'Dar placed his hands on hers, stopping their upward travel.

"Acise. Please. I cannot," and he turned his head away. Acise quickly withdrew her hands and stepped back, frowning.

Oh'Dar closed his eyes. *I have hurt her now. Quat!*

He went after her and spun her around to face him. He tried to block out how beautiful she was, the dark hair framing her face, her soft, pink lips.

"Acise. It is not fair to you. It is not that I do not find you attractive. You are beautiful. But we do not really know each other. I am not the boy that used to tease you by the fire. And you must know that I would be interested in pursuing this if I knew I was staying."

She slowly raised her eyes to meet his, stinging moisture welling in the corners.

"You are leaving? When?" she asked, blinking back her tears.

"I do not know. I think I am. I came here for a

short visit— I was only planning on bringing Kweeuu back. Now I do not know. But I cannot let myself develop feelings for you. I need to keep my mind clear right now."

"So you are saying if you let yourself get involved, I might keep you from leaving?"

"Yes. Of course," he said, looking down at her parted lips.

Without warning, she reached up and pressed her lips against his. He wanted to push her away, but she was soft, warm, yielding. Despite all his proclamations, he gave in and kissed her back, hard. His hands traveled down past her waist to the swell of her hips and pulled her into him. He lost himself in the delicious pressure of her body pressed up against his. His senses filled with the scent, feel, and warmth of her.

His heart pounding, he picked her up and started toward the sleeping mat. Her arms circled his neck, and she looked up at him willingly, running her fingers over his lips as he carried her. He had a general idea of what was to happen next, but right now, all he knew was that he wanted to press all of himself up against her—*hard*.

"What are you two doing!"

Oh'Dar spun around, placing Acise back on her feet by releasing the arm he had under her knees.

"Momma!" Acise called out.

"Both of you. *Come with me. Now!*"

Oh'Dar and Acise looked at each other, wide-eyed, and quickly followed Honovi out and down the corridor. She marched them over to the Healer's Quarters, where Adia and Acaraho were just getting Tehya settled.

Honovi stormed through the doorway with Oh'Dar and Acise in tow. She pointed into the room for them to precede her.

"I am *sorry* for the interruption," she said as Acaraho and Adia looked up suddenly. Tehya was already propped up on the mat Nadiwani had placed for her.

"But I just stopped our two *offspring* from—from —" Honovi turned away in frustration.

"Momma, I can *explain*," offered Acise, hurrying to Honovi's side.

Honovi turned, frowning, "There is *nothing* to explain. It was very clear what would have happened had I not stopped you both. Are you ready for this? Are you willing to make a commitment to each other? *Because you were sure acting like you were when I interrupted you!*"

Oh'Dar made tenuous eye contact with his father.

Acaraho stepped around Tehya's bed and over to Oh'Dar. He put his hands on Oh'Dar's shoulders, turning him, so the young man had to face him.

"What is going on, Oh'Dar? Are you and Acise *involved*?"

"I do not know—yes—no— *Probably*," he stammered.

"You either are, or you are not, son. Which is it?" Acaraho did not blink as he watched Oh'Dar's reactions.

"Yes," said the young man through clenched teeth, finally admitting to himself he had feelings for Acise beyond physical attraction. Her face lit up at his answer.

Acaraho turned to Honovi, who turned to her daughter.

"And you? Are you serious about Oh'Dar? Or are you just testing your powers?" she scolded. "Answer me, daughter."

Acise looked down. "I—I love him."

Honovi rolled her eyes. Adia's hand went to her mouth, and she shook her head. Acaraho saw Oh'Dar exhale and then avert his eyes.

"I think the *adults* need to talk," said Acaraho. "Please return to what you were doing. *Separately.*"

The two cleared out at Acaraho's orders. Tehya was taking it all in, knowing she would be a parent someday—hopefully.

Once the youngsters were gone, Acaraho turned back to the others.

"Do you think they would have taken it that far, Honovi? If you had not walked in?" Adia asked. Honovi shook her head.

"I do not know, Adia. I do know they have been

attracted to each other from the day Oh'Dar came back. From what I have seen, though, Acise has been the instigator. I cannot speak for Oh'Dar."

"I have seen him watching Acise. I know he is attracted to her. But I do not know if it is more than that. I would hope so, but—you know—he is a Waschini male who has recently spent a long time among his own people, so I cannot be sure of anything," said Adia.

"I know our cultures are different. You have strict rules about pairings, and he has been raised as one of you, but, as you say, he has been under the influence of the Waschini world for almost two years now. And in their defense, they are both tired," offered Honovi, now softening a bit.

"I watched his reaction when Acise said she loved him. I would say it is more than physical," added Acaraho, the only male in the room. "And they are of age," he continued.

Adia glared at her mate. "There's too much going on right now. Everyone is exhausted. We do not even know if Oh'Dar is staying or not. Something he said the other day makes me think he did not come home to stay."

She got up and started walking back and forth.

"Nothing would make me happier than for Oh'Dar and Acise to pair. From what you have told me, Honovi, there has always been a special connection between them. But when emotions and fatigue are leading, that is not the time to make life-changing decisions. I just want them to be sure. I do not want *either* of them to get hurt," she added.

Acaraho came over and pulled her into his arms. She buried her face in his chest and sighed, then inhaled deeply, breathing in his male scent.

"So, what do we do now?" Honovi asked.

"You do not have much choice," offered Tehya from below. "You have to trust them to make the right decision for themselves."

Acaraho looked down at Adia, still in his embrace. She looked up at him, and he smiled, raised his eyebrows, and tilted his head.

Adia looked over at Tehya. "You are right. They are both adults, like it or not. But I do pray they wait until things return to normal before making such a huge decision. I also wish Oh'Dar would follow our conventions, but I cannot force him."

Honovi nodded and then went over and hugged Adia as she stood in Acaraho's arms.

Soon after, Oh'Dar returned with the wolf pelt he had meant to bring for Tehya. He peered around the corner sheepishly before entering, head lowered.

"I am sorry. I wanted to bring this back for Tehya," he said, stepping in and covering her up with it. "You need to keep warm, Tehya, I am sure my mother and Nadiwani told you."

'Thank you."

Oh'Dar turned to leave, but Adia stopped him.

"Do you understand that we are not against you and Acise pairing if that is what you decide. Nothing would make any of us happier—your father, Honovi, me. We just do not want you two making a lifetime decision when you are both under so much stress. You need to spend as much time together as you can, assuming you can restrain yourselves. You need to find out if this is real or just a passing infatuation."

"I know, Mama. I do care for her, I admit it. I am glad you interrupted us, Honovi, because I would never want to hurt Acise by leading her on. I am not sure where my path is taking me, and until I know that, I cannot commit to her. Or *anyone*."

Honovi waited for Oh'Dar to continue.

"I never intended for us to be alone together. I should have left the minute I realized we were. I take full responsibility for what—almost—happened."

"Acise knows what she wants, Oh'Dar," Honovi said. "It is you who has to decide."

Oh'Dar scratched one eyebrow, nodded, and left.

Acise had run down the corridor after Acaraho ordered them out. Tears ran down her face as she fled. Looking for privacy, she had ducked into an empty room.

She leaned against the cold stone wall and let herself cry long, heartfelt sobs. *I love him. And I said it. But he did not say he loved me too. And what if he leaves! What am I going to do? There is no one like him— And those eyes—*

Oh'Dar needed time to think. On the way out of Kthama, he told the guard he was going to take Storm out for a ride and said he would be back shortly if anyone was looking for him.

Once down the rocky path to the valley below, Oh'Dar was finally free to let Storm run. The wind blowing through his hair was refreshing, and the crisp air filled his lungs. Their speed and the feel of Storm's muscles under him filled him with a sense of power and confidence. After a few good runs, he turned Storm back toward the Great River.

If it had been warmer, Oh'Dar would have taken a swim in one of the tributaries away from the current. He dismounted and stopped to let Storm drink. Then he lifted his face to the sky, and the sun breaking through the trees was warm and welcoming on his face after the cool air of before.

This is one of my favorite spots. How many hours did I spend here, swimming, floating, before I started worrying about what my future would be? This is where I found some of the first little shells and stones for Acise. Acise. What am I going to do about Acise? She said she loves me, but it could just be infatuation. She does not know me; I am no longer the boy sitting across from her by the fire. And I do not know her either.

What have I solved by finding my Waschini family? If anything, I am even more torn. There is no way to join these worlds, and I cannot live in both.

Storm raised his head from the shallow water. His ears pricked and his nostrils flared. Then he gave a whinny and shifted his hooves.

Oh'Dar brought himself out of his inner musing and listened. Nothing but the rustling of the leaves in the wind and the sound of the water cascading over the rocks. He picked out a blue jay in the background.

Storm startled again, his eyes wide.

Then Oh'Dar felt it too. The hair stood up on the back of his neck, and a chill traveled up his spine.

"Come on, Storm. Let us get home." He mounted and turned Storm toward Kthama.

Even after they were back, Oh'Dar could not shake the eerie feeling that he was being watched.

Nadiwani, still in Adia's quarters, was tending to Tehya. "You need to rest. It would be the best thing for you; build up as much strength as you can before it seriously takes hold. I am going to make you something to help you sleep."

She left Adia and Acaraho talking softly and returned in a few moments and gave Tehya something to drink. Then Nadiwani pulled the wolf pelt up over her and again told her to try and rest.

"I am going to go check on the others; I will be back later," and Nadiwani left the Healer's Quarters.

Adia turned to Acaraho. "Oh'Dar should have been stronger. I am disappointed in him."

"Do not be so hard on him, Adia. He is not one of the People. He is Waschini. He may have been raised as one of us, but it is not our blood in his veins. And he has spent time now in their culture, and we know little about their influence on him. If you notice, he speaks differently now. And it is one thing to resist a female who is behaving herself, but when she comes to you, making it clear she is willing, that is another. Do you not remember when you came to me that first night? All the years of self-control, even my training, meant I was able to hold you for hours when you were ill, pressed up against me under a pile of covers. But that night, when you made your intentions clear and offered yourself to me—"

Adia remembered Tehya sleeping on the other side of the room. She raised a finger to her lips, "*Sshh!*" she blushed. "That was not real!"

"But it was real. It was at the time, and it has been every time since. We both said what we shared in the Dream World was just as real as the times we have been together in waking life since," he reminded her.

Adia sighed. "*This* is why Healers should not have offspring. Or at least females should not. Maybe the Healers should be males—you all seem to have more objectivity."

"Well, not wanting to get into a debate with you, because I know I would lose, I think there is some truth to that. But it does not make either gender wrong. We just have different strengths, and I think each can learn from the other."

Adia recalled her father's words—balance. Balance of the three aspects—Mind, Will, Heart. *Hidden in every challenge is a gift,* she thought.

"Why are there not any male Healers?" he asked.

"You know; because males do not have the seventh sense," she explained.

"But if they did?" asked Acaraho.

"I do not see why not. We have never let gender restrict what any of us wanted to do or learn," she answered.

All the time she had been talking, he was running his hands over her arms, her back, down to her hips, pulling her close to him, stirring his desire for her. He lifted her face to his and kissed her softly. Her arms went up around his neck, and she leaned against him as he swept her up into his arms.

"Where are we going? To your quarters?" she laughed.

"Yes, apparently so."

"And you are going to carry me all the way there?"

"Yes, again."

"Like *that*?" she laughed, motioning downward with her head.

"No one will notice."

"Oh, I can certainly guarantee they *will*. What are you *thinking lately*?" For the first time, she wondered why only the females and the elderly males wore wraps for modesty.

He put her down, smiling. "Perhaps you are right. I will meet you there shortly," and he patted her behind as she walked past him, still chuckling.

As Adia stepped into the hallway, Khon'Tor was approaching, clutching something in his hand.

"I would like to see Tehya."

"Of course. Please, go in," and Adia moved aside. Khon'Tor entered the room, and Acaraho turned away, pretending to straighten one of the sleeping areas.

Khon'Tor went to Tehya and found her asleep, so he placed on her pillow the white feather he had found earlier, then stood a moment watching her. Her honey-colored hair splayed on the pillow, her tiny form barely raising the wolf pelts. Watching her breathing, he remembered their last carefree evening together; when she had proudly shown off her surprise to him, and the exquisite pleasure that had followed. Overcome with emotion, he turned away. On his way out, he handed Adia a small pouch.

"Please give this to her when she awakens. Tell her it is a surprise. She will understand. I had Oh'Dar make it for her and I was saving it, but—I would like her to have it now."

Adia nodded and went inside to set the little bag down on the work table. It was beautifully made.

It was late when Khon'Tor returned to his quarters. He stepped into the room and looked around. Empty. Desolate. Everywhere were reminders of Tehya. Her wrappings were lying near the bed from the last time they had lain together, and her scent hung in the air. He ran his fingers through his silver crown and stared at the empty rooms.

This is what it would be like if something happened to her. I cannot stay here.

Khon'Tor left Kthama.

He took one of the paths into the valley below, anger building higher with each step.

This is your fault, Hakani. You had a second chance. We both did. And yet you knowingly brought sickness to all of us. And now she is ill. If anything happens to her, I swear— Please, Great Spirit, please do not let losing Tehya be my punishment for what I did. I accept that I deserve to be punished, but do not make her pay for my crimes.

Uprooting a young oak, Khon'Tor tossed it against a rocky outcropping, where it splintered and crashed to the ground, sending pieces of dirt and wood everywhere. He leaned over to grasp a granite boulder and jerked it up. He lifted it overhead and dirt and leaves dropped onto him as he did. Using all his strength, he heaved it into the center of the river, spray from the impact drenching him in return. He lifted a fallen log and swung it at a stand of other trees, pulverizing them on contact. Wildlife scurried in all directions. He stormed about; boulders, trees, logs—whatever he could get his hands on—became a means to dispel his rage.

Then, out of breath and finally spent, he dropped to his knees in the soft loam, slumped forward, and hid his face in his hands. More than almost anything, he wished Hakani dead. Her being here had brought back a rage he had thought was gone. *I will not go back to being what I was. I cannot, for Tehya's sake.*

Khon'Tor threw back his head and let loose a visceral cry of anguish that echoed through the dark sky. At Kthama, heads lifted as far inside as the Great Chamber.

That evening, as he had done so many years ago, Khon'Tor, Leader of the People of the High Rocks, found his familiar place, stretched out his full eight feet, and fell asleep under the cold canopy of twinkling stars.

CHAPTER 7

Days passed. As many of the People recovered, so as many more fell ill. Nadiwani started feeling faint, and before long, she was bed-ridden herself. Adia now had two in her quarters to nurse back to health.

Tehya was not improving—not as Adia wanted. She and Oh'Dar kept her warm and dry, Adia bathing her as needed to keep her comfortable. Oh'Dar replaced the wolf pelts regularly, washing them out between uses in one of the shallow eddies of the Great River, then drying them near the outside fires.

When Tehya woke up, Adia gave her Khon'Tor's present.

"Khon'Tor stopped by earlier when you were sleeping. He did not want to wake you, but he left you that white feather, and this," and Adia handed Tehya the little pouch.

Tehya opened it gingerly. She reached in and brought out a necklace. She held it up to look at it.

"Oh—" she exclaimed, letting it dangle and twist in front of her. "From Khon'Tor? How? Why?" She laid back down, exhausted from that brief period of sitting up, her necklace clasped carefully to her heart.

Oh'Dar answered, "He wanted to give you something special. To thank you—for being his."

Then he continued, "It was after you gave him your surprise. He asked me to make it for you, but he picked out all the stones himself. You can see he matched them to each other perfectly."

It was a beautiful work of art. Amethyst, carnelian, and amber were sewn into a beautifully woven chain of the finest sinew she had ever seen, with a larger polished amber stone at the center. It complimented her coloring perfectly.

"I wish you could have seen him, that huge male so focused, patiently picking through the stones," said Oh'Dar.

Tehya started to cry. Adia bent down and put her arms around the young female for a while. Then she looked up at Oh'Dar, her eyes pleading for him to have a solution.

Oh'Dar paced, futilely wracking his brain.

When Tehya had calmed down, Adia got up to talk to Oh'Dar quietly. "Is there any chance that Nadiwani is re-infecting her?"

"I do not see how, Mama. After all, I have been

here as long as anyone, and I have not caught it again. And none of the others who have recovered have relapsed either. All we can do is keep her warm and dry and keep fluids going through her. However, she does not seem to want to eat, and she was thin to begin with. I admit that worries me."

"I agree. We have to get her to eat; maybe Khon'Tor could help. Oh'Dar, please go and find him."

Oh'Dar returned with Khon'Tor more quickly than Adia had expected. The Leader looked over at his mate lying on the mat, her figure a tiny bump under the wolf pelt. His eyes widened as he realized how thin she had become. He had to turn away.

Adia put her hand on his shoulder. "She is still holding her own, but she needs to eat. Perhaps if you sit with her, she will eat for you."

Khon'Tor pinched the corners of his eyes with his fingers and nodded.

"Tell me what to do."

Adia led him over and sat him down next to Tehya. Much like Acaraho had done for her after Khon'Tor attacked her, the Healer lifted Tehya so that she was sitting propped up against her mate. Oh'Dar brought over a bowl of warm bone broth, and they gently woke Tehya. She lifted her face to see Khon'Tor holding her.

"Khon'Tor!" her arms slipped up around his neck immediately. Despite all his restraint and to his great consternation, tears threatened to slide down his face.

He discreetly wiped them away and then looked into her eyes. "Sareste'," he whispered, "You have to eat. Please."

She shook her head.

"Yes. Just try it."

She shook her head again and closed her eyes.

"Tehya," he said quietly. She buried her face in his chest.

Wrong approach, he thought.

He put his hand under her chin and lifted her face to his. She opened her eyes. Staring at her, he said, "Now listen to me. You *will* eat; this is not your choice. You belong to me, and you will do as I say. I will not put up with your defiance. You will obey me."

He did his best to be stern, and even though it had only ever been part of their lover's play, it worked.

Tehya nodded and took a little of the broth. Oh'Dar and Adia both sighed in relief.

Deep inside Khon'Tor, the pleasure of having her surrender to his orders surfaced once again.

He stayed as long as it took to get the entire bowl into her. When it was empty, he handed it to Adia and lay back down, moving Tehya over to rest against him. He circled his arms around her protectively, her tiny body lost in his.

Adia remembered again how Acaraho said he had done the same for her when she was recovering from Khon'Tor's attack.

She and Oh'Dar checked on Nadiwani, who was asleep, and then left the room to Khon'Tor and Tehya for a while.

They returned later that evening. Adia was pleased that Khon'Tor was able to get another bowl of broth down Tehya.

"Khon'Tor, if you need to leave, I can lie with her," Adia offered.

"No," he said.

"If there is *any* chance this is helping, I will stay."

Adia nodded. Tehya did have a light covering, lighter than most of the rest of theirs. It was possible that Khon'Tor's body heat was playing a role. But she suspected it was his presence that was comforting Tehya and making the difference.

Morning found Khon'Tor still curled protectively around his mate. Adia noticed a change in her breathing and that she was sleeping more soundly than before. She was glad to see that Khon'Tor had also gotten some rest.

Adia was also relieved to see that Nadiwani was

improving as well, and more quickly than Tehya. Oh'Dar was now making broth for both of them.

Khon'Tor stirred and woke, sitting up while trying not to wake Tehya. He looked around as if getting his bearings. "How is she this morning?"

"Doing better; her breathing is clearer, more even. She seems to have slept more soundly with you here," Adia answered.

"Should I wake her to eat?"

"No, let her sleep. Oh'Dar will re-warm the broth when she does wake."

Khon'Tor looked around uncomfortably. Adia could see he needed to get up but probably did not want to leave Tehya alone.

"It is fine, Khon'Tor, I will be with her. It will not hurt her if you are away for a while."

Khon'Tor hoisted himself up and went over to get a drink. Standing at the work counter and sipping from a drinking gourd, he turned to Adia and Oh'Dar.

"Thank you, Adia. For everything. Thank you, Oh'Dar." His face was still tight with concern for Tehya.

Oh'Dar spoke first. "You are welcome, Khon'Tor. I am glad I can contribute. It was hard to leave Kthama, but I learned a lot while I was away."

The Leader suddenly looked more serious still. "Oh'Dar, tell me why you left. I need to know."

Oh'Dar looked away. "I do need to tell you and the others more about where I have been and what I have learned. There just does not seem to be time," he answered.

Adia noticed that her son had not answered the question.

Oh'Dar continued, "I know you have a lot on your shoulders, Khon'Tor, but the more time you can spend with Tehya, the better. She needs to eat. I wish she had not lost so much weight; she does not have it to spare. She is doing better, but she is not out of the woods yet. And we cannot promise that, even if she recovers, she will not lose the offspring."

Adia froze. *Oh no. No. Oh'Dar, no.*

The drinking bowl slipped out of Khon'Tor's hands and smashed into a thousand pieces on the stone floor.

"Offspring? *Tehya is with offspring?*"

"Oh, I thought you knew. She did not tell you?" Oh'Dar looked at his mother, wild-eyed.

"Tehya is seeded? With my offspring. How long? *How far along is she?*" Khon'Tor practically roared.

"I would say about five months. She hid it well, being so thin to begin with. But she has lost a lot more weight."

Adia rushed to Khon'Tor and grabbed his arm. "Listen to me. *Listen to me.* Oh'Dar is speaking very cautiously, trying to prepare you. So far, everything is fine, and you are getting her to eat now, so we are hopeful. But the most important thing is Tehya. She is young. If worst comes to worst—"

She stopped herself. There was no real way to rationalize that losing an offspring was something one could move on from—

"*Take care of her*. Hakani will pay for this," and Khon'Tor was gone in a flash, the sound of his footfalls filling the corridor.

"Mama, I am so sorry." Oh'Dar was shaking.

"You did not know that she had not told him. Just go and find Acaraho. Quick. *Now!*" she ordered.

Oh'Dar shot out in search of Acaraho, maneuvering as fast as he could through the winding stone tunnels, clumsily slamming into the stone side walls and pushing back off, still keeping his momentum going, still not moving anywhere as fast as Khon'Tor.

The Leader of the People of the High Rocks was on the move. He ducked into Oh'Dar's workshop, and Honovi startled as he called out, "Go to the Healer's Quarters to help care for Tehya. *Now!*"

Khon'Tor continued on.

He turned down the corridors, bursting into the living quarters. Empty. There was only one other place they could be. He stormed up the corridor to the Great Chamber. Everyone in his path jumped hastily out of the way as a combination of searing rage and expert trajectory barreled him down the passageways.

Stopping when he entered, Khon'Tor's eyes quickly swept the room. He spotted Hakani, and every head turned as the Leader stormed toward her, arms outspread.

"*Why did you come back? You did this.* You knew Akar'Tor was ill and you knew it would spread. We gave you our help, a second chance, and you repaid us with what? Lies and *betrayal.*"

Then Khon'Tor turned away. He pressed his fists to his forehead.

When he turned back, his eyes were cold with rage. "After everything you did to destroy me, it was still not enough. How much hatred can one soul embody? Tell me!"

Those in the crowd looked around confused, trying to figure out what was causing their Leader's outrage.

Khon'Tor picked up a stone table slab within reach and hurled it against the far wall, shattering it to pieces. The sound echoed through the Great Chamber. Everyone in the area ducked and ran for cover from the flying splinters.

"So help me, Hakani—if she dies, *I will kill you.* And this time, there will be no possibility of your coming back!"

Everyone froze and turned to look behind Khon'-Tor, who swung around to see Haan edging toward him, half crouched, eyes narrowed.

Khon'Tor swung back around and tossed rock benches, overturned tables, and threw everything else out of the way to clear space behind him.

Alerted by the noise, guards streamed into the Great Chamber and lined up along the sides. Receiving no acknowledgment from Khon'Tor, they scanned the huge room looking for either Acaraho or First Guard Awan to give them orders to engage.

With one swing, Haan cleared the side to his left. People scrambled to get out of the way of the flying boulders, rock slabs, and pieces of stone.

The Sarnonn snarled and motioned angrily for Hakani and Akar'Tor, who stood blankly next to her, to move out of the way.

Everyone watching knew that Khon'Tor, as impressive as he was, did not stand a chance against the Sarnonn. At over twelve feet tall and twice the bulk, Haan towered over Khon'Tor. His biceps bulged as he clenched his fists. A growl curled his lips, revealing razor-sharp canines the size of the Brothers' arrowheads. All eyes stared at him; now angered, he was a behemoth killing machine.

Oh'Dar and Acaraho came bolting around the corner just in time to see Haan and Khon'Tor face off.

With two steps, Acaraho was at Khon'Tor's side, and the Leader slipped him a fleeting glance. Acaraho nodded in the direction of the guards, but Khon'Tor quickly raised his palm face-up, a command that they stay put. Within moments,

Oh'Dar had joined his father. Everyone in the crowd gasped; it was a show of support and little else. There was nothing Oh'Dar could contribute— Then another figure joined them, as Nootau lined up. Khon'Tor and his contingent stood facing Haan; eyes locked, hackles raised.

The remainder of the males in the room were picking up whatever they could find to use as weapons, moving in front of the females and offspring.

Haan looked at them all and roared, the ear-splitting sound echoing through the Great Chamber. Khon'Tor and the others braced for his onslaught as the Sasquatch took a step forward.

Adia came skidding around the corner to stop next to Hakani and Akar'Tor. Her heart missed several beats at the sight of Acaraho, Nootau, and Oh'Dar standing with Khon'Tor against Haan. Her hands flew to her mouth.

My entire family, nearly everyone I love, is going to be slaughtered in front of my eyes.

Adia took a step forward. "Please. Please do not," she pleaded, not knowing if Haan could hear her, lost in his concentration on the battle about to take place.

Haan took another step toward them, and Adia slumped to her knees sobbing. "Great Mother, *please.* They are all I have."

Suddenly, there was an abrupt movement as another figure darted into the fray, landing directly between the two warring factions, facing the menacing Sarnonn.

Tall, muscular, determined, his palms raised, he stood in defiance of the angry mammoth figure towering a few feet in front of him.

"Father. No. *Stop!*"

It was Akar'Tor.

Haan growled and swept his arm sharply to the side, motioning Akar'Tor to get out of the way.

"*No!*"

Akar'Tor kept his hands raised, palms facing Haan, and took a step toward the hulking giant.

"*He is my father!*" He pointed to Khon'Tor.

Haan signed back then pounded on his chest, "*I am your father!*"

"Yes. Yes, you are my father. You raised me, and I will always be your son first. But *he is also my father.*" Akar'Tor's hands sliced the air harshly.

Haan paused, his chest heaving, eyes still pinned on Khon'Tor. The Sarnonn looked at the resolve in his son—also Hakani and Khon'Tor's son—whom he had raised as his own, and their eyes locked. Still maintaining his position, Haan clenched and unclenched first one fist and then the other.

Eyes darted as Akar'Tor spoke to Haan in Sarnonn. "Think of Mama. Please."

Adia leaped to her feet and ran to Akar'Tor, putting her arm around his shoulder. Khon'Tor and Acaraho exchanged fleeting glances.

Acaraho gritted his teeth and swore under his breath, "By the Mother, *Adia*."

Everyone in the room was frozen in place. Time stood still as they all waited for the next move. Khon'Tor and Acaraho did not dare move or speak. The more time passed, the greater the chance that emotions would fade and reason would return.

Haan straightened, abandoning his offensive posture.

But at the next moment, Hakani let out a cry and doubled over.

In one leap, Haan was at her side. Adia ran to them and squeezed around Haan, putting a hand up to tell him to let her in to see.

Hakani was folded over in pain, and Adia soothed her forehead. She needed Hakani to stretch out so she could feel her belly, but the female would not uncurl; the pain was too severe.

Adia looked up at Haan, "Carry her, gently now, easy. Follow me." Haan cradled Hakani gently to his chest and carried her along behind Adia.

Akar'Tor turned to face Khon'Tor before following them. Their eyes met. For each, it was like looking into a mirror. Then, without a word, Akar'Tor took off after his parents.

The moment they were gone, the crowd started moving back into the middle of the room. The males went to righting the rock tables and benches, setting off to the side those that were broken. The females comforted the younger offspring and started cleaning up what debris they could.

Khon'Tor, Acaraho, Nootau, and Oh'Dar remained in the center of the room, oblivious to the flurry of activity around them.

"Akar'Tor did not owe us that," said Acaraho.

"I am not sure he did it for us. But there is no doubt that he saved our lives," said Khon'Tor, and he finally noticed all the activity around them as the community members repaired the damage he and Haan had caused. He turned to Acaraho, who was staring down the tunnel into which his mate had disappeared with the Sarnonn.

"He will not hurt her, Acaraho. He knows she helped Akar'Tor and that she will help Hakani. But as soon as possible, we need to reconvene."

"I agree. But I wish to check on Adia regardless, and depending on what transpires, the Healers may need a rest before we meet."

Oh'Dar called back as he sprinted away, "I am going to check on Tehya and Nadiwani."

"I will be along in a moment," Khon'Tor called out after him.

Adia did not like moving Hakani, but she could not help her where she was. Taking her to the Healer's Quarters, where Tehya was recuperating, was out of the question.

Within a few minutes, Haan was placing Hakani on the worktable in Nadiwani's quarters. Adia took one of Haan's hands and placed it on top of Hakani's head and showed him how to make easy strokes, hoping to sooth Hakani. Hakani moaned, her hands covering her extended belly.

Adia did her best to examine Hakani while the female was doubled over. *I cannot tell anything with her curled up like this. But whatever is going on does not matter—time is running out either way.*

She said a silent prayer and turned to look at Haan. His eyes were filled with concern, and worry creased his heavy brow. The earlier anger was gone, replaced only by a look of anguish. Searching his eyes, Adia thought, *I have to find a way to communicate with him without any chance of misunderstanding. I have to make him understand the offspring must be born now; that they will both die otherwise. And I cannot assume Hakani has made this clear to him.*

Based on what we just witnessed, the Sarnonn may not be naturally aggressive, but when angered, they are no more in control of their emotions than any of us. If the worst happens, he has to understand it is not our fault. If not—

She had moments to decide. The vision of the three males she loved lined up across from Haan, about to be slaughtered, flashed through her mind again. It was a terrible risk, but risk was all she had right now. If it worked, it worked. If it did not—they would all be dead soon anyway, no doubt.

Adia asked Haan to move Hakani over to a mat on the floor, not wanting to risk her rolling off the examination table while they otherwise occupied. Then she took Haan's hand and had him sit down across from her, a safe distance from Hakani.

"Haan, please trust me. I will not harm you, I promise, but Handspeak is too slow. Will you open your mind to mine? With no secrets?"

Haan hesitated at first, but strangely, he seemed to understand what she was about to attempt. Sitting cross-legged in front of him, she tried to push from her mind the fear triggered by his monstrous size. She reached for his hands and curled her own around two of his fingers. It was the best she could do. She closed her eyes and shifted her consciousness. A window started to open between them.

Adia focused her own thoughts inward. She prayed for help, and help came. She sensed Urilla Wuti's consciousness reaching out to hers. *Why is Urilla Wuti joining me?*

She stopped the Connection and looked at Haan, squeezing his fingers to get him to open his eyes.

"Do you understand? May I do it again?" she wanted to know if he understood what she was doing.

Haan nodded for her to continue.

Adia closed her eyes once more and re-established the Connection. The window started to open again, and this time she did not stop it. She could feel Urilla Wuti's presence with them, shoring Adia up but holding herself separate. *I have so much yet to learn,* was Adia's last thought as herself alone.

Adia bore down on the opening, trying to keep the focus narrow. But she had never encountered a Sarnonn before; everything she knew of them came from stories and fables. She felt herself being sucked into a maelstrom; the more she resisted, the stronger the draw became. Her concentration collapsed, and Haan sucked her consciousness into his own.

She felt it shred into fragments then come back together, interwoven with his. There was no more separation between the two. She was him, and he was her, and their memories intertwined. Laughter, joy, grief, horrific pain tossed her emotions and thoughts around like leaves in a churning tempest. She was huge and powerful. Incredible strength coursed through her. There was nothing she could not do. And she was alone, isolated, suffering. A female, a mate, who died in her arms. Grief; unbearable grief over not being able to save her. Tenderness. Love. She remembered finding Hakani floating on the decaying log, clinging to life. She gently lifted the semi-conscious form from the stream, water dripping, and carried her home. Back in the confines of their shelter, the anxious days that passed before the female gained consciousness. Other females in his pod providing her with care. Akar'Tor and the joy in their community at the birth of an offspring, even though not one of their own. Earlier days of hunting with the other Sarnonn. A glimpse of Ageless secrets before a door slammed shut, shrouding them somehow from her knowledge. The Great Mother. An offspring's memories. His first kill. Then a great wall rose between them, and she could go no further. And then the Connection was gone.

Adia shook her head, straining to bring herself back. She knew she needed time alone to process this. It was overwhelming. Nothing like she had encountered before, not even with Urilla Wuti.

Adia put her hands to her face, realizing she was shaking. *What the krell just happened? The Sarnonn's seventh sense abilities must be far more developed than ours. Thank the Mother that, from somewhere, Urilla Wuti realized my distress and broke the Connection. I would not have had the strength to pull myself back out.*

She knew that as much as had transferred to her had transferred to him. But how much? *Does Haan now know everything? I have so much to learn. It seems I do not always have the control I need to have over this! Or else the Sarnonn have these same abilities at much stronger levels. I initiated the Connection, but he took control of it immediately. Of course! I am not thinking clearly. In a way, we are both Sarnonn, but the People have the Brothers' blood in us.*

Hakani moaned, and Adia tried to get up. She was unbalanced on her feet and faltered, but Haan reached out and steadied her.

Their eyes locked.

Intelligence. So much intelligence here. The Sarnonn are not inferior to the People; the stories are wrong. We did not leave them behind *when we bred with the Brothers.*

Haan rose with Adia and asked, "What can I do to help?"

Adia had read his Handspeak. It usually looked clumsy to her and was difficult to understand, but in her mind, she had heard him speak clearly and fluently. She brushed it off as her imagination until he asked again.

"Healer, tell me what you need me to do. I love her, and I cannot lose her, despite everything she has done," said Haan.

There was great sadness in his eyes—more than the moment warranted. Adia realized that Haan now knew everything that she did; how Hakani had put Oh'Dar's life in danger, how she had spoken against Adia in the High Council, how she had stolen Nootau to kill him. Her hatred of Adia. And yet Adia realized that Haan still loved Hakani, and for that, the Healer was grateful. *I wonder if he now knows the reason for Hakani's jealousy of me; that I was Khon'Tor's First Choice.*

"I did not know all she had done to create the problems here," Haan added, eyes downcast.

"Stay with her, Haan. I have to get help; I cannot do this alone. I will be back as soon as possible, I promise." Adia flew out to find someone—nearly *anyone* at this point.

Oh'Dar had returned to his mother's quarters and was relieved to see Honovi and Acise there. Tehya and Nadiwani were sleeping soundly. Oh'Dar had an idea and ran back to his workshop.

Acaraho came to find Adia and they crossed paths as Adia was on her way to Nadiwani's quarters.

He grabbed her hand, and she slowed down. "I only have a moment," he said. "I must hurry. Are you alright?"

"Yes. But what happened back there? Who started it?"

"Khon'Tor was screaming at Hakani, blaming her for Tehya's being ill. Haan took offense at his mate being threatened—"

Adia shook her head, "I have to go, find me later!" She turned and continued racing down the corridor.

Within moments she appeared in Nadiwani's quarters, out of breath. "I need you, Honovi. Can you come? Or Oh'Dar—where is Oh'Dar?"

"He just left; he said he was going to his workshop and would be right back."

"How are they doing?" Adia asked hurriedly, glancing down at the two patients.

"Both sleeping well at the moment. What is going on?"

"Oh, I wish Ithua were here. There just are not enough of us to go around. I have to induce Hakani. It is time."

Honovi and Acise looked at each other, both

unconsciously inhaling deeply and breathing out slowly.

"I can stay here with Tehya and Nadiwani," said Acise. "Oh'Dar will be back in a moment." Seeing the look on her mother's face, Acise added, "It is alright, Momma. I promise I will behave."

Honovi flew out through the door with Adia to Nadiwani's quarters.

They found Haan sitting on the floor next to Hakani, tending to her. She was still balled up in discomfort. Honovi went over to the supply area to find what they needed.

"Black Cohosh? Red Raspberry, or Licorice Root tea?"

"I do not think we can get tea in her at the moment. But Black Cohosh, yes. And we will need a pile of clean wraps."

Adia turned to Haan and signed, "We have to make the offspring come now, Haan. If we do not—"

Haan nodded. He understood. He had felt Adia's worry and concern during the transfer. As the females worked, Haan was himself trying to recover from their Connection. Never knowing her mother who died giving her life, having to leave the Deep Valley to become the Healer for the People of the High Rocks. Learning, studying. The loss of her father and her desperate regret at not being there for him. Acaraho. But the worst of it for him was Hakani's betrayal and cruelty. Hakani kidnapping Oh'Dar as a tiny offspring and displaying him dangerously for all the community to see. Hakani standing at the cliff edge, planning to kill Adia's son along with herself. Adia begging for his life and Hakani's cold refusal to spare him. And then, most recently, her abject terror at the thought that he, Haan, was about to slaughter nearly everyone she loved.

So little of what Hakani had told him was the truth. But he would deal with that later. Right now, the female he still loved, in spite of what she had done, might be dying.

The Healer got the Black Cohosh into Hakani and waited.

"It is not enough. I need Cramp Bark, Squaw Vine—" Adia pressed her palms to her forehead and paced.

"Ithua has both. I will go."

"No, I need you here. Who else can we send?"

"*Acise*—I will send Acise; she can ride!" offered Honovi.

"Where *is* Acise?"

"She is with Oh'Dar looking after Tehya and Nadiwani. Before you say anything, we agreed that they have to spend time together."

Right now, thought Adia, *I am not going to think about Oh'Dar and Acise being alone together. I am not sure that Oh'Dar even knows how to mate. He has not been through the Ashwea Tare, and as far as I know, he has never accidentally walked in on any of the paired mates. But from what I do know, the Brothers are not so strict about secrecy around the mating act, and Acise may even have experience.* She continued, "It would probably be best to send Oh'Dar. He has already had the sickness and recovered, so he should not be contagious. And that stallion of his is no doubt faster than any of the ponies."

Honovi nodded and was off.

Left alone with her thoughts, Adia wondered where Khon'Tor and Acaraho were. *Most likely staying away, not wanting to stir up more trouble. Oh, Khon'Tor, what were you thinking, facing off with Haan like that? But you were not thinking, were you; you were panicked at the thought of losing Tehya and your offspring.*

And what is going on with Hakani's offspring? Adia covered Hakani up. *Nothing to do now but wait. And pray.*

Oh'Dar had returned to Adia's quarters by the time Honovi got to them.

"I need you to go to Ithua and ask for some supplies. Tell her what has happened and what we are doing. Hakani's offspring must be induced now.

We need Cramp Bark, Squaw Vine—whatever she has. She will know."

Before he left, Oh'Dar gave Kweeuu his command to stay. The grey wolf went over and curled up next to Tehya.

Oh'Dar happened to encounter Khon'Tor on his way.

"I am going to Ithua to get some supplies. I will be back as soon as I can."

"How is Tehya?"

"She is sleeping soundly at the moment."

Khon'Tor nodded. "I will leave her be for now. I will be back later."

Before long, Oh'Dar was mounted and off. The sound of Storm's hooves pounding the path from Kthama echoed up through the Great Chamber.

Khon'Tor had ordered Acaraho to put plans together to sequester everyone possible—in either their own quarters or their gender groups. If things went the wrong direction and Haan became violent, Khon'Tor wanted as few of his people around as possible. Acaraho had dispatched Awan, Mapiya, and the others to carry the word. The guards were still at their posts, doubled where possible, and still bearing spears.

Oh'Dar rode as hard as he could, but Storm was not used to the rocky terrain, so he had to trust the stallion to set the pace; a fall could be fatal for them both. Luckily, dawn was just breaking. However, even on Storm, it took a while to reach the Brothers.

Is'Taqa was meeting with Chief Ogima when the sounds of heavy hoof beats broke into the morning air. Braves ran to meet the potential threat; it was not one of their ponies because the cadence meant a longer stride. Either it was the Waschini, or it was Oh'Dar on Storm.

Oh'Dar came flying down the incline. Finally on level ground, he pulled the stallion to a stop, dismounted in a flash, and ran toward Is'Taqa and Chief Ogima.

"Chief Ogima, Is'Taqa. Forgive me for my abrupt entrance, but where is Ithua? I need help. Hakani is seeded by the Sarnonn, and my mother needs to induce labor," he said.

The two Chiefs were dumbfounded. "Hakani is with offspring, by a *Sarnonn*?" asked Is'Taqa.

"Yes, please. I will come back and tell you more later. I just need Ithua."

Is'Taqa turned to his daughter, Snana, who had been stringing beads next to him. "Go and find Ithua. Quickly. Like the *wind*, Snana."

Within moments Snana returned with Ithua. Oh'Dar explained in detail what was going on, following her as she gathered her supplies.

He rattled off about the appearance of Haan,

Hakani and Akar'Tor, the fever, and the altercation between Khon'Tor and the others with Haan that almost ended in their deaths.

"Hakani is carrying a Sarnonn offspring?" She frowned and shook her head.

"I need to go with them," she announced to the two Chiefs.

"No, Ithua, you cannot," interjected Oh'Dar. "That will leave no one here with your people because the sickness is still active. If you come, you will not be able to return for some time; you could bring it back with you, and Honovi and Acise are already trapped at Kthama for the same reason."

"I realize that is the risk. But if things go wrong with delivering that offspring early and the Sarnonn blames the People, from what you have told me, if he becomes irrational, there is no telling how many innocent people may be harmed. For the sake of the People, Adia needs all the help she can get right now to make sure the offspring survives being born early. It is a question of the greater need. She would accept the risk for us if the situation were reversed."

Ogima Adoeete nodded his agreement and signaled with his Chief's stick for someone to bring her a pony.

"While I am gone, please start everyone on Echinacea. Snana knows where it is kept, and it is already divided into individual doses. There should be enough for everyone for several days."

"Can you ride behind me?" asked Oh'Dar as he mounted. "Storm will be faster."

Ithua nodded and ran off, returning in seconds with a long strip of leather. She mounted Storm, lashed herself to Oh'Dar, and then wrapped her arms around his waist.

"If there is an emergency, alert one of our watchers; if need be, someone will come," Oh'Dar called out to Is'Taqa and Chief Ogima.

"Go," said Ithua, and Oh'Dar kicked Storm into action.

I hate to run Storm so hard without a break, but it cannot be helped. Though if he has a heart in him like Dreamer, he will be fine.

Oh'Dar felt as if they were moving in slow motion, though he knew they were not. Ithua's presence comforted him. *Surely with all the knowledge between them, the offspring will be fine. If not—is this why I was brought back here? To watch everyone I love be killed before my eyes? Surely that cannot be the reason. We could do everything right, and the offspring could still die. It will not be fully developed, and it still has to be able to nurse. I do not know how things could be worse.*

As soon as they arrived back at Kthama, Oh'Dar found one of the guards to take Ithua to Adia, and they took off through the winding hallways. "I must take care of Storm," Oh'Dar had called after them, "I will be along as soon as I can."

Adia looked up when Ithua entered Nadiwani's quarters and ran over to embrace the Medicine Woman the moment she saw her.

"Oh, I cannot believe you came; thank you! But you know that you will have to stay for a while now? Or you will risk taking this terrible sickness back home." Adia was speaking through tears of gratitude and relief.

"I know; it will be alright. How is she doing?" Ithua looked around for Hakani and stopped cold when she saw Haan.

Through the ages, with the People becoming the dominant strain of Sasquatch in their region, the Brothers were not sure there were any still around. They had become the stuff of legend. And now, here was one looming before her. Against her will, her heart pounded in her chest. *Despite what Oh'Dar said took place, they are said to be peaceful. They are supposed to be non-violent*, she tried to convince herself.

Ithua tore her eyes off Haan. *Later.* She busied herself examining Hakani. "What have you given her so far?"

"Black cohosh. It is all I had. So far, it has not taken effect."

Ithua nodded and tried to get Hakani to sit up, but could not.

"We need to give her something to relax. How far along is she?" Ithua asked.

"We are not sure, truthfully."

Ithua nodded. *Could it be worse? Inducing an offspring of unknown development, sired by this hulking giant—who is also a nervous father with the strength to wipe out practically the entire community if he turns on us. No idea if the offspring will be able to nurse even if it does survive. Sickness everywhere else and not enough help. Perfect.*

Honovi was already going through the satchels, looking for what they needed. "Which first? Squaw Root or Cramp Bark?"

"Both."

Knowing Haan was watching, Honovi and Adia made sure not to look at each other, even though Ithua was ordering twice the medication necessary.

Honovi tightened her jaw, prepared both, and administered them. They waited. It did not take long. Hakani moaned and clutched her belly.

"Haan, it is time. We need you to step outside."

"No. I am staying."

Honovi and Adia looked at each other; males were not permitted to be present for birthing.

"We do not have time to debate. If you are going to stay, then we will use you. Help her over to the birthing stone, please, then help support her from behind. Here, I will show you," said Adia.

Haan did as Adia instructed and knelt behind Hakani, easily supporting her in place.

Hakani moaned.

Supported by Haan, Hakani's water broke and

contractions rippled through her belly. "Hakani. Do not push. *Not yet.*" Ithua ordered, smoothing her forehead. *Too soon*, thought Ithua. *She is not ready.*

Time moved slowly. More contractions. Hakani became more conscious and better able to cooperate. Fortunately, this was not her first offspring. Unfortunately, the offspring was still half Sarnonn.

Finally, it was time, "Push Hakani, *push hard*," instructed Ithua.

Hakani screamed and pushed, breathed, and pushed again. Finally, one painfully loud outburst later, Adia was holding a wet, squirming offspring, a female. Even though she was premature, she was the size of one of the People's full-term offspring.

Haan helped Hakani over to the sleeping mat, and Adia placed the newborn on Hakani's chest. Hakani cuddled her offspring close, and she looked up at Adia with tears in her eyes.

"We are not out of the woods yet, Hakani," whispered Adia. "She still has to be able to nurse. If she is too young, there is not much else we can do. Time will tell now."

Hakani nodded and looked down at her daughter. The offspring had more of the People's features than she had expected. She had prepared, telling herself it did not matter what the offspring looked like; it was hers. And Haan's. But she could not hide her relief that the little female favored her more than Haan.

Adia told Haan that he had a daughter. He

reached out to touch the offspring but drew his hand back.

"You can touch her, just be gentle," said Hakani.

"I wish I could tell you everything is fine, Haan, but I cannot yet. She still has to be able to nurse," Adia said. Haan nodded and went over to sit on the floor and leaned against the wall. Adia, seeing that Ithua was attending to Hakani and the offspring, joined him. They sat quietly together and waited.

Adia was exhausted. The mental and physical stress were taking their toll. She could not remember when she had last eaten. Or when she had last seen Acaraho—except back in the main eating area when she thought Haan was about to kill them all. She needed rest, and she had yet to process her Connection with Haan. But she did not dare leave until they knew the offspring was going to nurse. Propped against the wall, she was asleep within minutes.

Adia awoke wondering where she was. She was warm and comfortable. Suddenly she sat up with a start. She had fallen asleep next to Haan and slumped over. He had let her rest against him, not waking her. She blinked and looked for Ithua, who came out of the other room holding the wrapping the offspring had been in. Adia's heart stopped.

Ithua saw her widened eyes, "No, no. It is fine,

Adia. I just changed wrappings; the offspring is fine. In fact, she is nursing."

Adia eased herself to her feet to see. *Now, if only she can drink enough. If only she has the strength to do so.*

"I think you should find Acaraho and rest for a while. We are fine here," said Ithua. Adia thought for a moment. There was nothing keeping her there. If something happened to the offspring and Haan flew into a rage, her presence would have no effect in stopping him. She looked back at the Sarnonn before she left. Having made a Connection with him, the possibility that he might hurt any of them seemed very remote now.

"Haan, I am going to find my mate. Will you be alright if I leave?" she asked. Haan nodded and motioned for her to go. "I will have some food brought to you," she added before she left.

It was all Adia could do to keep walking; she so wanted to rest, to clear her mind. If she could have tolerated another Connection, she would have sought out Urilla Wuti's counsel, but the strength of Haan's will, once the window opened, had swallowed her into himself, and she could not. Had Urilla Wuti not broken it off, Adia doubted she could have. *I have to contact Urilla Wuti as soon as I am able. I need to understand what happened.*

As she walked back, Adia remembered Haan's words about Hakani after the Connection, "*I love her. I cannot lose her, despite everything she has done—*" So whoever had said it was right; the story Hakani had told him was not the truth.

As soon as this calms down, I need to talk to Khon'Tor.

Acaraho came around the corner at the same time Adia did. He caught up both her hands. "Are you all right?"

"Just worn out. The offspring was born, and she is nursing, too. That was our other concern. Now it is a matter of time to see if she can take in enough nourishment to survive. What have you been doing? Oh, and Ithua came."

"We have a lot to catch up on. You look exhausted; are you up to a meeting?" Acaraho asked.

"Yes, we need to meet. I made a Connection with Haan."

Acaraho frowned. "You mean like you did with me?"

"Yes, in a way. I was wrong about them. Well, at least him. I took his clumsy Handspeak as an indication of his intelligence, and I was wrong. He is as intelligent as we are, that is for sure. But there is more; there is something else about them. I need to sit with it before I can put it into words."

"Khon'Tor doesn't know you have this ability?" Acaraho asked.

"No. The few of us who can do it do not talk about it openly, Though Urilla Wuti's Leader knows about it. Hakani lied to Haan, and when I can sort it out, I can probably figure out how much and about what."

"It does not surprise me. Who knows, she might even have told Haan that Khon'Tor pushed her off that ledge."

Adia nodded. "I need to sleep, to clear myself of this, and I cannot go to my quarters."

Acaraho said, "Let us go to mine. I will go with you and help you get settled."

"I need to send some food to them. They have not eaten."

"I will take care of it."

Acaraho escorted Adia to his quarters and then had food and water delivered to Nadiwani's. Other than the armed guards, the corridors were eerily empty. Khon'Tor's directive was in force.

CHAPTER 8

Tehya and Nadiwani had woken long enough to eat and be washed. It would still be some time before they were up and about, but it was going in the right direction, and that relieved both Acise and Oh'Dar who were tending them.

As promised, Acise had not teased or flirted with Oh'Dar. And true to his word, he also did his part to keep everything on a platonic level. They did work so well together, and her lightheartedness helped him deal with the pressure.

For some reason, Khon'Tor has been turning to me for guidance. He never paid me any mind before, but since I returned, much has changed. Maybe it is him, or maybe it is me. Whatever it is, I do not want to let him down, and I do like having something to contribute.

"Oh'Dar?" Tehya was awake. "Where is Khon'Tor?"

"He came earlier to check on you, but you were asleep and he only had a moment. I am sure he will be back soon, though. How do you feel?" He crouched down next to her, placing the back of his hand against her forehead.

"I ache. And I am so tired. Where is my necklace?" she asked, trying to look around. But she had to lie back down.

"Right here. In the little pouch next to your pillow. Let me get it for you."

"Put it on me, please. I want him to see I am wearing it when he gets here." Oh'Dar shook the necklace out of the pouch and helped her sit up enough for him to put it on. Within minutes she was asleep again.

"What was Khon'Tor like before?" Acise had a lot of questions, but Oh'Dar did not mind. As long as they were talking, he was not thinking about kissing her.

"He was always a powerful Leader. Strong. Confident. Driven. He never faltered in knowing what to do. He would listen and assess a situation and then make a decision. The People trusted him. That part has not changed, but he is softer now. No, that is not quite right. He is more open now. Like with Tehya; he does not always hide how much he loves her. Before he would not have wanted anyone to know—because it would have made him—vulnerable."

"Did he love Hakani like that? What happened between them?"

"No one truly knows but them. There always seemed to be tension from what I heard. But did he ever love her like that? Oh, I do not think so. This is a once in a lifetime love, I think, what he and Tehya have. As far as Khon'Tor and Hakani are concerned, toward the end, from what I have learned over time, it seems they outright hated each other. I imagine he was relieved when he thought she had died. It solved a lot of problems. She hated my mother, though I still do not understand why. There is quite a story there, I am sure."

"Nothing interesting happens at our village," she said, looking down at her work.

"Oh, well! You should come and live here; you will never be bored!" He chuckled, but immediately wished he had not said that.

An awkward silence fell. Moments passed.

Just then, Khon'Tor arrived. He greeted Oh'Dar and Acise and immediately stepped over to Tehya.

"How is she doing?"

"Much better. Please wake her; she has been asking for you," said Oh'Dar.

Khon'Tor crouched down, preparing to sit, and then suddenly jumped back.

"What the—"

Thump, thump, thump. Kweeuu wagged his long tail under the wolf pelts, lifting them up. He popped his head out from under at the top edge and looked at Khon'Tor, his tongue hanging out.

"That was smart, Oh'Dar," Acise smiled at him.

"What you did with Kweeuu. Using him to keep Tehya warm." Oh'Dar tried to suppress his pleasure at her admiration.

Tehya rolled over, threw an arm over the grey wolf, and sighed. Kweeuu looked as if he was smiling.

Khon'Tor glanced over at Oh'Dar and shook his head.

"I had to improvise, and I think she likes him there. He is keeping her very warm."

Khon'Tor had to smile at the ingenuity.

"Tehya," he whispered. She turned away from Kweeuu and opened her eyes.

"Khon'Tor." She unwrapped herself from the wolf and put her arms up around Khon'Tor instead.

"Well, I am glad to see you prefer me over that thing."

"He is not a *thing*, Adoeete. He is a wolf. And he has a name. It is Kweeuu. Try to pay attention," she teased.

Khon'Tor breathed a deep sigh of relief; she was feeling well enough to give him a hard time. He lay down and pulled her against him, the gravity of the situation making him careless of what Oh'Dar and Acise might think. He brought his lips close to hers but stopped short of kissing her.

Oh'Dar and Acise looked at each other. Acise blushed.

"Will you two be alright alone for a little bit? We have not eaten all day. Nadiwani was just awake and ate, so she should be asleep for a while," stammered Oh'Dar.

Khon'Tor raised his hand without taking his eyes off his mate, then returned to caress her face. "Go. And take your time coming back."

Oh'Dar called Kweeuu, who dragged himself out from under the covers and trotted after his master.

"I hope I am blessed enough to have someone love me like that one day," said Acise under her breath.

Khon'Tor arranged the wolf pelts back over Tehya, who was now snuggled up against him. Nadiwani was sleeping peacefully on the other mat. He listened to Tehya's even breathing.

What would have happened to her if Haan had killed us all today? Would she have taken a different mate? Of course. She is young and beautiful and kind. Any male would want her. Krell, they have probably already pictured her under them. The idea of anyone else mounting her, even thinking about it, makes my blood boil.

And I almost got us all killed today. I cannot let Hakani affect me like that. I have to be above it. I do not have the luxury of losing control. Acaraho stood with me, and so did Oh'Dar and Nootau. I must not forget that. The Great Spirit is blessing me in ways I do not deserve. Tehya, Adia's forgiveness, the loyalty of others.

I should also find out what is going on with Hakani's seeding. What about Tehya. Our offspring? No—do not think about that now. She is going to be fine. That is all that matters.

Khon'Tor's mind was now spinning with fatigue. Tehya stirred and moved closer, but he did not want to sleep. He had too much on his mind and wanted to drink in the moment with her lying innocently next to him, clinging to him for comfort. *I would do anything to protect her. I would give my life without hesitation.*

He looked down and noticed she was wearing the necklace he had asked Oh'Dar to make for her. Khon'Tor pulled her a little closer; he cherished the feel of her in his arms. Despite his intentions, he fell asleep within moments.

Mapiya offered Oh'Dar and some of the others a place to stay after he and Acise had gotten something to eat. Now daybreak filtered through the overhead ventilation shafts.

Oh'Dar woke and stretched and got his bearings. Kweeuu was lying next to him, keeping his back warm. Cold air drifted down with the sunlight, and Oh'Dar realized that he had been away from Shadow Ridge since the warmer weather.

What are Grandmother and Mr. Jenkins thinking? I need to get back—but how can I leave now with so much

*going on? I wish I could write to them and tell them I am
alright.*

He sighed. *All this time and I still do not know where
I belong. I am not one of the People. I am not one of the
Brothers. I am not even truly Waschini. There seems to be
no place for me in the world.*

Oh'Dar shivered; it was chilly. *I need to make
proper winter wraps if I am going to stay much longer;
how could I forget how cold Kthama is. It is getting hard
to move around, clutching all these extra layers. I must
make something warm that is easier to wear. I wonder if I
can work alongside Honovi and Acise in my workshop?*

Kweeuu pawed at Oh'Dar.

"Alright, let us go. I need to find out what else is
happening, anyway." Oh'Dar stepped carefully, not
wanting to wake Mapiya or the others. Nimida and
Acise were lying on mats on the far side. Nootau was
lying on one closer to Oh'Dar. *Females to the left,
males to the right, Mapiya smack in the middle.*

*Nimida and Nootau seem to be getting close. It makes
sense; the High Council chose them for each other after
all. She seems nice enough; I wonder what Mama thinks?*

*In the Great Entrance, as he was taking Kweeuu
outside, a*n icy blast hit Oh'Dar in the face, suddenly
bringing him fully awake. Kweeuu romped in the
snow as if it were nothing, biting at the snowflakes as
they fell. At times he still seemed like a cub. Oh'Dar
pondered how, for some reason, Kweeuu had fallen
in love with Tehya the minute he met her, wallowing
all over her feet and begging to be petted. Many

nights he slept outside their quarters, much to Khon'Tor's chagrin when he had to step over the wolf as he left. Oh'Dar knew Kweeuu would keep Tehya warm and was glad Khon'Tor was allowing the wolf to remain with her.

Awan stopped Oh'Dar as he came inside. "Your father wants you to meet him in Khon'Tor's meeting room after you have eaten."

"Just me?"

"No, all of us—those who are available. Khon'Tor, your mother; Tehya and Nadiwani if they are well enough, and you, as we did before. I am now looking for Khon'Tor."

"Nadiwani is still sick; she will not be coming. Neither will Tehya. If you see my father, please tell him I will be there as soon as I can, but I need to check on them. Khon'Tor may be with Tehya, and I will tell him you are looking for him, and where we will be meeting."

Awan nodded and went on to let Acaraho know. Before long, they were assembled again.

"Before we start, I want to hear updates from all quarters. First—what is the status of Hakani's seeding?"

Adia spoke, "Ithua is here with her. We induced the offspring, and she is holding her own. She is nursing, which was the next hurdle. I am cautiously saying that we could not have hoped for a better outcome. Haan is calm and with them."

A daughter. Khon'Tor suppressed the urge to ask

which the offspring favored—the Sarnonn or the People.

"You know how Tehya and Nadiwani are doing, but I will update the others," said Oh'Dar. "Both are coming along, being able to stay awake for longer periods of time. I expect each to make a full recovery, but it will still be a couple of weeks before they are back on their feet. Tehya has lost a lot of weight; weight she did not have to spare, I might add. Anything to get food in her is a priority. Honovi and Acise help Ithua, but also continue to prepare their medicine and take care of those in the care areas in Nadiwani's absence," he finished.

"Yesterday, I ordered everyone to stay sequestered in their private or communal areas in anticipation of Haan's reaction should the birth not have gone well. At this point, it sounds like I can lift the restriction," said Khon'Tor. "The sickness has already spread, for one thing."

"Based on what I now know about Haan, I do not think there will be another incident, Khon'Tor," said Adia.

"Based on what you know? What have you learned, Adia, and how?" he asked.

She pursed her lips. "I cannot tell you how I know this, Khon'Tor, but he is deeper than we thought—than I thought. And I mistook his remedial Handspeak as a reflection on his intelligence. But he is just as intelligent as any of us. And he does love Hakani and Akar'Tor."

"You cannot tell me how you know this? Or *will* not?" Khon'Tor was direct.

"As a Healer, there are things I cannot disclose."

Khon'Tor did not press further. *So I am not the only one with secrets.* "What else can you tell us about them?"

"As strong as they are physically, they are equally strong in spirit. And there is something more that I cannot get my mind around. A grounding, a rooting. A greater, far more powerful connection to the Earth and the Great Spirit than we have. It is almost as if their essence is woven into the strands of creation that make up Etera herself. Somewhere along the way, we lost that—or at least most of it compared to the abilities they possess."

Oh'Dar frowned at her statement.

"Perhaps that is how they stay so well hidden. After all, we had no idea they lived so close to Kthama. Had Hakani not come looking for help, we might never have learned about their existence," she added.

Acaraho added to Adia's statement. "That makes me question how reliable our reports are. If they are that good at concealing themselves, there could be pockets—even whole communities—of them anywhere. It would be good news if they are better established than we think—but it also means that finding them will be even harder than we thought. But why stay hidden all these generations? Why the secrecy?"

"Perhaps Haan will help us after all of this is over. If we explain the situation—" Adia stopped, remembering that this was a High Council topic and that Oh'Dar and Awan had joined them.

Khon'Tor interrupted hastily, "We are getting into other matters now. Let us postpone those for now.

"Make no mistake; we are no match for the Sarnonn if they were to come at us in numbers. Now that we know they exist, it goes without saying that we must ensure peace between us. We do not know how many are in Haan's community. We have to accept that there may be other populations of Sarnonn as well, if not in our proximity, then close to our other communities. Whatever happens, none of the lives of the People will ever be the same.

"At a closer level, I do not pretend to know what will happen once Hakani and her daughter are well enough to travel. She said she would return to Haan's people. My hope is that they will do as she says. The sooner that happens, the sooner we can stand down the armed guards placed throughout Kthama," added Khon'Tor.

"What about Akar'Tor?" asked Oh'Dar.

"What *about* Akar'Tor?" asked Khon'Tor.

"He is your son by Hakani. He is a potential heir to your leadership."

"He is my son, but in name only. He has been raised by the Sarnonn, and he knows nothing of our culture. He may carry my blood, but he has no framework from which to lead our people. You would be better able to take my place, Oh'Dar. You are more one of us than he could ever be."

Khon'Tor was just making a point, but from Oh'Dar's delighted smile, he could see it meant something more to the young man. *As hard as I have been on him, as much as I have rejected him, Oh'Dar still values my opinion of him.*

"It is a strange twist of fate. Your son is now in the same position I have been all my life. An Outsider. How will he find his place with them? Who will *he* take for a mate when the time comes? Maybe he will want to remain at Kthama, in the same way that I left to find a home with the Waschini." And Oh'Dar lapsed into thought.

"Save your sympathy for someone who deserves it," snapped Khon'Tor. "Akar'Tor will never be one of the People. His mother ruined any chance of that for him long before he was seeded."

Adia could bear it no longer. She took a deep breath and asked, "What *are* your plans, Oh'Dar? I know you cannot leave right now, but what are you going to do? Are you staying or going back to the Waschini?" She held her breath.

Oh'Dar pinched the bridge of his nose, then sighed. "I came here intending a short visit. I had to bring Kweeuu back. How he tracked me there all that way, I will never know—and to a place where I had not been living for several months. I thank the Great Mother he did not track me farther into the Waschini's world; he would have been killed for sure.

"But even as I came back, I felt there had to be a reason other than that. And here we are. I hope I have added value. But beyond that, after we are past this, I do not know. I have my feet in two worlds now."

"Three, to be accurate," said Acaraho.

"Acise," admitted Oh'Dar.

"Who is Acise?" asked Khon'Tor.

"Acise is Honovi and Is'Taqa's eldest daughter. She came with Honovi. Acise and Oh'Dar have—developed an attraction for each other," explained Adia.

Khon'Tor nodded his head. He had recently thought that the Waschini would have to take a mate from the Brothers. Now he understood Acaraho's remark.

"Oh'Dar. For what it is worth, I hope you will stay." It was as close to an apology as Khon'Tor could make. He changed the subject quickly.

"How close is the sickness to running its course? Are you able to give me an estimate?"

Adia replied, "Another two months or so."

Oh'Dar nodded in agreement. He added, "All the Brothers' Healers are with us. It is not wise for them to be without a Healer, but we cannot let Ithua and Honovi go back until we are more confident it has passed. It would be better if they come down with it now. But, we do not know what the incubation period is, and they could still take it back with them even if we thought it had died off," added Oh'Dar.

"If that is true, and because there is no way of knowing how long this remains contagious, then it does not matter when they go back. We are still guessing. As you said, we cannot keep them indefinitely. But in the meantime, can we send Nadiwani, so they are not left with any help? Once she is well enough? At least she will have had it and recovered." Khon'Tor suggested.

Adia nodded. "She would have to stay out of sight, in case the Waschini ride through, Though it is unlikely; it has been so long since we last saw anything of them. But it would give her a chance to learn about the Brothers first-hand. It is a good solution, Khon'Tor, provided Chief Ogima Adoeete agrees. Thank you."

Khon'Tor took a moment to think; a snarled up bundle of thoughts were tumbling around in the back of his mind. *We need an even closer alliance with the Brothers. The more we intertwine, the easier it will be to garner their support—if it comes to that. Even though the High Council said our blood is already too mingled, it may be our only choice. We do not have access to any Waschini, and Oh'Dar hardly counts. Before they leave Kthama, I also need to see what Hakani's offspring looks like.*

He spoke again. "Adia, what else can you tell me about Haan and his group? Do you know how large it is, how many are there—and how they live?"

Adia had seen flashes when she and Haan were connected. "I can tell you that they are fairly well established, but only about a third of our numbers. They live underground, as we do."

"There is another Kthama?" Awan joined in finally.

"Yes, to a point. It is not as large, and the entrance is not through the rocks like Kthama. The entrance is at ground level, and it goes down farther. And Haan is not just one of them, Khon'Tor; Haan is their Leader. Your counterpart, their Adoeete."

Dead silence.

"That explains a lot. Perhaps that is why he could take one of the People as his mate. But why? Unless —" Acaraho's stopped; they were bordering on topics the High Council had ordered confined to the High Council members.

Khon'Tor stood up. "If there is nothing else in general, Oh'Dar and Awan, you are dismissed. The rest of you will stay," said Khon'Tor.

Awan and Oh'Dar looked at each other, frowning at the abruptness, but got up and left as told.

Acaraho sighed. "Maybe it is not just Haan and Hakani. Is it possible that the Sarnonn know about Wrak-Ayya? Why else would a Sarnonn take one of the People as his mate? I doubt that we are any more attractive to them than they are to us."

"We have been ignorant to think they do not. We share the same root. If the story of Wrak-Wavara survived with us, it could well also have survived with them. Not all the Sarnonn took part in the

Wrak-Wavara because they still exist as a separate people," surmised Adia.

"So it is possible that having made contact with us, Haan is now considering taking his people down the same path we are looking at? Their community may well be facing the same issues we are; running out of safe pairing combinations. So when he found Hakani, the opportunity came to cross-breed. But why wait so long after she got there?" said Khon'Tor.

"I can answer that. Hakani may be many things, but she is not stupid. She had to know that she would be risking her life. From what she told me, she held him off until recently. In the end, she felt she owed it to him. I doubt it was pleasant," she added, then blushed. "But I find it hard to accept that Haan would intentionally have endangered Hakani's life for an experiment."

"Despite the risks, the High Council meeting must take place. This is new information. The opportunity is here to make an alliance with the Sarnonn. We need to bring them into the discussion." Khon'Tor shook his head and ran his hand through his silver crown. "And I just made a mortal enemy of their Leader."

Adia responded to Khon'Tor, "I do not think so. Haan was reacting to your attacking Hakani. He was protecting her. I doubt he would have been the aggressor had you not gone after her, so I am sure you can make amends

In the past, he would have railed at Adia's criticism of him. Instead, Khon'Tor appreciated that they were all speaking frankly. *I will never be able to be around Hakani without getting angry. Too much history together. Too many unresolved injustices.*

"Does he understand that you had to force the offspring to be born before it was ready? Do they not have Healers among their ranks?"

"Yes, he knows I had to induce the offspring. As far as Healers go, I do not know the answer to that. If they do have Healers, they must not be as knowledgeable as ours, or Hakani would not have sought us out. Akar'Tor was also sick when they came, remember."

"Akar'Tor's situation must feel untenable to him," said Acaraho. "The son of two Leaders—the People's by blood and the Sarnonn by family. Yet he can never rule over either. He truly has no place—even worse than it is for Oh'Dar in some ways. Akar'Tor feels some allegiance to us—or at least to you, Khon'Tor. He stopped Haan from slaughtering us all."

Acaraho paused. "Depending on how they see him, Akar'Tor may hold the key to our future relationships with Haan's people, perhaps as some type of intermediary."

"If Akar'Tor holds the key to our future relationship with Haan's people, then the cause is lost before it has begun," stated Khon'Tor. "I will never accept him."

"Has anyone seen Akar'Tor?" Acaraho asked.

They looked around the room at each other, uncertain.

Akar'Tor raised his face and let the falling snow help clear his mind. He dusted himself off and stood, scanning the horizon to look for a break in the clouds. He was tired of being cold, but not ready to return to Kthama. He disassembled his temporary shelter and smothered what was left of the fire. He had not needed it as much to keep warm, as that the light comforted him. And he needed comfort now—

He thought about going back to the Sarnonn. He could be there in a few days. *I want to go home, but what about Mama? Did she have the offspring? Is it alright? I will have to go back to Kthama first and find out. She and Father must be worried by now. I have abandoned them both.*

He was the son of Khon'Tor, Leader of the People of the High Rocks. He was also the son of Haan, Leader of the Sarnonn tribe. And yet he belonged to neither.

Akar'Tor looked up at the sky again. He kicked the embers to scatter them, then ran his hand through the silver shock that mirrored that of Khon'-Tor. *All right. I need to go. I am not going to find answers out here.*

He picked up his things, pulled his shoulders

back, and turned around to trudge up the path to Kthama.

"I have not seen him since the stand-off with Haan yesterday," said Adia.

Acaraho pursed his lips and shook his head no, "I have not either."

"Since we are on the topic of offspring, there is something I would like to discuss while it is just the three of us. Khon'Tor, may I speak freely?" she asked.

Khon'Tor had to chuckle, "Have you ever *not*, Healer?"

In spite of the tension, Acaraho also smiled.

Adia began, "I am worried about Nootau and Nimida. They are spending too much time together. They seem to be growing closer and closer. The High Council paired them, and it has to be in the back of their minds that they 'belong' together. I do not know what to do. I do not know if Nimida is established enough to bear the truth, but I cannot let this continue between them."

"I have seen it too," said Acaraho. "Like it or not, Adia, it is time to tell her. To tell them both."

"I saw her looking at Nootau, then at Akar'Tor. I thank the Mother that Nootau does not have your silver hair, Khon'Tor. I cannot tell you how long I have feared its appearance. Seeing Akar'Tor, it seems that Nootau will never develop it, since it has not shown by now, and he is past maturity," said Adia.

Khon'Tor unconsciously ran his hand along his crown, an indication that he was struggling with something or about to make a decision.

"All of this is my fault," he said in a moment of disclosure.

The three remained dead silent.

Nootau and Nimida did not know they were brother and sister. Nootau thought his father was Acaraho when, in reality, it was Khon'Tor. Khon'Tor was also Nimida's father. And they were half-blood siblings to Akar'Tor. All of them were of pairing age —yet neither Akar'Tor nor Nootau could be paired with Nimida.

No one but the High Council, Nadiwani, and the three of them knew this secret.

"Nootau will be hurt and angry. He will blame me. And blame Acaraho, too—they both will. There is no justification for having sent Nimida away unless we tell her that you are her father and how she was seeded. I have tried to think of one, but the only reason is the truth—which we cannot reveal," and Adia dropped her head in defeat.

"I have no answer for you, Adia, as far as this convoluted mess with Nootau and Nimida is concerned. I have no solution unless you are asking me to take public responsibility for—"

Khon'Tor braced himself inwardly, counting his

breaths as he waited for the outcome of his calcu-
lated bluff.

"No, Khon'Tor. The risk to the community is still
the same. We will have to bear this burden a while
longer and pray that the Great Mother will make a
way at the right time." She sighed heavily.

*I know her so well. My gamble paid off. If she wants
to reveal what I did, she will still be the one to bring
everything down on our heads. After all this time of
silence, the risks are even higher should this truth become
known. I may possibly tell Tehya someday, but it will be
my decision, in my time and no one else's if I can help it.*

*And, though Adia may be back to holding her silence,
I have no influence over Hakani.*

As if reading his mind, Adia continued, "And
Hakani—what are her real intentions? I keep going
back and forth about her. I am sure she does not
trust us any more than we trust her. She was never
one to take responsibility for anything, and I am sure
she still blames you, Khon'Tor, and me, on some
level. She also knows the truth about Nootau. Hakani
could break this wide open if she wanted to."

Listening to this, Khon'Tor thought again of
Tehya. His precious Tehya. *What would she think of
me if she found out the truth this way? On top of all the
other problems, the only true happiness I have ever
known is now even more at risk.*

He was back to his original question about
Hakani; *Did she come here only to get help for Akar'Tor
and her unfortunate seeding?*

"We cannot solve this with the information we have now," he said finally. "We need to know more. We need to find out where Akar'Tor is, for one thing. And we need somehow to determine what Hakani's real goal is. And we need someone to get close to Haan," he said.

"I have already established a relationship with Haan," said Adia. "I will take that on instead of Nadi-wani or Oh'Dar, as we considered earlier. I will find out if the Sarnonn know about the Wrak-Wavara. Hopefully, if they are looking to mix their blood with ours, he now realizes that it has to be the other way. A male Sarnonn cannot seed one of our females, but I can speak for our females and say that none of them would be willing to be seeded by a Sarnonn male anyway, given a choice. Hakani only did it because of affection built up through the years, and possibly a sense of obligation."

"I can speak for the males and say the same. I do not know any who would want to bed a Sarnonn. *Given a choice*." He added, "If they want to conquer us, Khon'Tor—"

Khon'Tor nodded. In a full-blown battle between the Sarnonn and the People, depending on their numbers, the People would ultimately lose.

"We will meet again in a few days. In the mean-time, Acaraho, find out if your watchers have seen Akar'Tor. Adia, you continue building a relationship with Haan. It is fair to say none of us can befriend Hakani, so we have to work through him. If you can get any insight into Hakani's true intentions—good; otherwise, see if he knows about the Wrak-Wavara. But do not jeopardize a chance to connect with him, if you have to choose.

We will send Nadiwani to the Brothers as soon as she is well enough. As of now, we will let the High Council meeting stand as scheduled. Anything else?"

They shook their heads. "All right then. That is all." And Khon'Tor dismissed the meeting.

Khon'Tor headed off to see Tehya. He knew that Adia and Acaraho had been staying in the High Protector's quarters since theirs had been turned into a care station for Tehya and Nadiwani. Honovi and Acise looked up as he came in.

"You just missed Oh'Dar, Khon'Tor. He was here checking on them." Khon'Tor went over to his sleeping mate and crouched down next to her. She stirred and opened her eyes. "Adoeete," she said. Ever since he had told her never to use the honorific, she had taken delight in using as much as possible.

As she rolled over, he noticed she was wearing something different. He lifted the covers, "What's this? Another surprise?" It was a light cotton shift, something Khon'Tor had never seen before. Tehya smiled, "No, it is just something Oh'Dar made for me. He made a few in different colors. It is for a little bit of extra warmth under the covers."

Just then, Oh'Dar returned, carrying two similar creations.

He looked up to see Khon'Tor and said, "Oh, you discovered what I made for Tehya."

Khon'Tor stood slowly, eyes locked on Oh'Dar the whole time, his muscular arms crossed high on his chest.

"And just how did you know they would fit her?" he asked.

"Oh, no, Khon'Tor. Acise helped me. She did the final fitting on Tehya. Not me. I just thought, since Tehya— Since she said she was feeling either too warm or too cold under the covers—" Oh'Dar's voice trailed off. He shot a nervous look at Honovi and Acise.

"Oh, Khon'Tor," interceded Tehya, "Please. He only meant it to help." Then to break the tension, she added, "I am sure you can still figure out how to get me out of it if need be."

"Trust me, Tehya. Getting you out of that thing is hardly a concern. When you are feeling better, I will be glad to demonstrate."

Honovi turned to Acise and Oh'Dar, "Out, out!" And after shooing them through the door, she followed them down the corridor; it seemed that Khon'Tor and Tehya had better have some privacy.

Once they were alone, Khon'Tor returned to his position next to Tehya, leaned in, and gently touched his lips to hers. She placed her hand on the side of his face, her eyes sad.

"Khon'Tor, I am so sorry. I have let you down. I lost your offspring," she said. Tears welled up and spilled over. "And mine. My little one. Whom I will never get to hold or comfort. Whose smile I will never see."

He sat down and pulled her over to him, bringing her into his lap. She wrapped her arms around him, and he held her while she sobbed. "I am sorry; I am so sorry. Adia told me that Oh'Dar slipped up and told you I was seeded before I could. I was not keeping it from you; I just wanted to be sure."

He stroked her hair, "You have done nothing wrong, Sareste'. And you have not let me down."

He pulled her back to meet his gaze.

"We have years and years to make offspring, Tehya. I am not in a hurry; we are still getting to know each other. If it had happened, that would have been fine. But I am happy to have you all to myself for a while longer."

She nodded, then buried her face in the soft mat of his chest hair, her warm tears still soaking into the curls.

"What have you eaten today?" he asked.

"Some broth. And fruit. Honovi has been bribing me to eat." She tried to smile.

"Bribing you? With what?" he asked, smiling.

"Mostly only with promises so far. But when she gets back, she will collect them for me, shells and agates. They find them in the creek beds where she lives. She saw the necklace you gave me, and she said she could get me some more stones if I liked."

"Ah! So that is the key to your heart," he said, glad the subject had changed. He could not bear to see her cry; she was so vulnerable to begin with.

"Oh no, there is only one key to my heart, my Adoeete. And you have it." She looked up at him, tears still slipping down her face. She gave him a soft kiss and laid back against him, curled in his lap.

He sat and held Tehya. *When this is over, I have to make it up to her. Somehow. Thank you, Great Spirit, for taking care of her. Thank you that she was safe here when Haan—* Khon'Tor's thoughts returned to his altercation with the Sarnonn and his anger at Hakani for bringing the sickness there. *No matter what, I have to keep her out of this.*

He picked up an edge of the cotton shift and rubbed it between his fingers. He did not remember seeing anything so lightweight. Oh'Dar was right; she did need something a little extra at night. *Next subject* Khon'Tor said to himself, thoughts wandering to when she would be well enough to give herself to him again.

Khon'Tor's reverie was interrupted by footsteps coming to the door. "I am sorry to interrupt you, Adoeete. But we have a visitor. Two people are traveling along the Mother Stream."

"Who is it, Awan?" he asked.

"I do not know the names of the other. But one of them said her name is Urilla Wuti."

Adia and Acaraho lay stretched out together, talking in his quarters, Adia with her head on Acaraho's shoulder.

"What else did you learn about the Sarnonn?" he asked.

"There was so much information at once. I am still sorting it out. Haan is their Leader, though I did not get the impression that their community is as structured as ours. He had another mate before Hakani. Or rather, coinciding with Hakani. She died not too long ago. I got the impression that is why he waited so long to mate with Hakani. He was broken-hearted when his mate died. For some reason, they never had offspring, which they call *offlings*. Their cave structure is similar to ours, except that it goes deep underground, as I said. That is all I can tell you for sure. Other than that, as I said, he does love Hakani."

"You said that you think she did not tell him the truth."

"He said that he loves her, *in spite of what she has done*, or words to that effect."

"It does not surprise me. I would hardly expect her to be honest about her role in the difficulties with Khon'Tor.

"You said the offspring is holding her own. Is she going to survive?" he asked.

"Yes. I believe so. Ithua has been with them constantly, with help from Honovi and Acise.

"I am tired, Acaraho; could we sleep now?" she asked.

"Yes. Let us get some rest. There is no guarantee that tomorrow will be any easier."

Adia laid her head back down and scooted closer to Acaraho. Just as she was about to drift off, her eyes flew wide open, and she sat up straight.

"Acaraho. Urilla Wuti is here."

Acaraho groaned. He did not want to get out of their warm bed; they had so little time together anymore. "You mean here, now?"

"Yes. I have to get up."

He flipped off the bed covers, "I will go with you."

CHAPTER 9

Urilla Wuti had traveled to the High Rocks along the Mother Stream, the life-giving river which ran underground and connected several of the People's communities. Her companion carried her satchels, indicators she would be staying a while.

Adia embraced her. "I am so happy to see you. But Urilla Wuti, you should not be here. There is a sickness; so many of us are ill, and you have walked right into it. Nadiwani is recovering in the Healer's Quarters. She is there with Khon'Tor's mate—his new mate," she added.

"It is fine. I am not concerned. I see you weathered your last storm well, and I thought for this next one, I would give you some help."

This *next* one?" Adia bit her lip. *When does it ever stop? And why help with this one? Why did she not help me last time?*

But, instead, she said, "It is late. Let me get you to some quarters; a good night's rest will help all of us, and if you are going to stay, you must promise me not to overdo it, and you must minimize your contact with anyone who is sick." She paused. "Oh, and Urilla Wuti—the Sarnonn, Haan—there is so much to tell you that I do not know where to start."

Acaraho looked down at the small, wizened Healer. "It seems there will be much to talk about tomorrow. Let us now get you settled and comfortable," said Acaraho.

Adia hugged Urilla Wuti and watched her leave with him.

Standing outside the door where the older Healer would stay the night, Acaraho said, "Tomorrow I will make more suitable arrangements, but these quarters will get you through tonight. Your companion will be just down the hall. How long are you staying, Urilla Wuti," he added.

"I do not know, Acaraho, but it is good to see you again."

The next morning found Urilla Wuti and Adia deep in conversation in Urilla Wuti's temporary quarters. The older Healer wanted to hear everything that had happened between her, Khon'Tor, and the High Council during the Ashwea Awhidi.

Adia sat and told Urilla Wuti how Nimida had

come to the pairings and that she and Nootau had been chosen for each other. She explained how she had told Kurak'Kahn, the Overseer, that they were brother and sister. That the Overseer had asked Nootau to revoke his request to be paired, and that when he did, Khon'Tor had unknowingly claimed his own daughter for his mate.

Through all of this, Urilla Wuti sat quietly, hands folded in her lap, and listened without saying a word.

"I asked for a High Council meeting to set aside Khon'Tor's claim over Nimida on the basis of the problems between him and me. But they upheld his authority to select her. Urilla Wuti, I snapped. All the years of the lies and protecting him, to come to what? Khon'Tor mating his own daughter? They were revering him and disparaging Acaraho after all these years, during which Acaraho took the blame. I exposed Khon'Tor, that he was the father, that he had taken me Without My Consent."

Adia gazed blankly for a moment. "Anyway, he admitted to it. All of it. He did not even try to defend himself. The High Council was going to banish him, so I— I withdrew the accusation."

Urilla Wuti nodded, knowing what that meant. "So Khon'Tor is free. And no one other than a few of the High Council members know that he, and not Acaraho, is the twins' father?" she asked.

"Yes. But something I cannot explain came of it all. After that, everything changed. He changed. We all changed. And the battles that raged between us are gone as if they had never been—" Her words trailed off.

"Adia, what did you expect of the High Council when you turned to them?"

Adia stood up and paced around.

"I expected them to have *answers*. I expected them to come up with a solution that would not destroy our community. Banishment? There is nothing worse; you know that. When I was speaking to them, I felt powerful. I was speaking the truth, and it was healing to get it all out, finally. I believed that truth would set things right. But it did not."

"Are you sure it did not—ever?" Urilla Wuti asked.

"No, it did not. Well. Maybe. If you look at the fact that the war between us is over. And we are working together, instead of against each other. But the High Council did not help at all. If anything, their solution would have made it worse. I protected Khon'Tor all those years because of what it could do to the People. But their decision would have caused even more harm. We would never have recovered. Not only could there have been civil war among our people here—but they could also have turned against the High Council. Our entire order at High Rocks would have been destroyed, with potentially far-reaching consequences that would also affect the other communities. In times of crisis, people need someone to believe in, someone to lead the way. Is bringing one person to justice worth causing so much harm to so many others?"

"So, who resolved the problem?" Urilla Wuti asked.

"I suppose I did when I withdrew my charge against him."

"So the answer did come, it just did not come from where you expected; the High Council. You gave the High Council the power to provide a solution, and they did, even though it could have destroyed the High Rocks and caused bloodshed. And, yes, word would have spread to other communities. But when you took the power away from them, it was you who provided the way out for everyone."

Adia sat back down next to Urilla Wuti and looked down. "So why could this not have happened years ago? Why all these years of struggle and battle between us?"

Urilla Wuti put her hand over Adia's. "Answer your own question, Healer."

Adia sighed. "Because it was not time. Because neither Khon'Tor nor I were ready; he had to learn to surrender his power, and I had to learn to claim mine."

"All Leaders understand that there is a time to wield the blade and a time to lay it down. Those who become great are those who develop the wisdom to know when to do which," said the older Healer. "And for how long," she added.

Adia looked back up at Urilla Wuti, leaned forward, and whispered. "And you could not help me with learning that?"

"You had to find your own power, Adia. You could not have done that leaning on me."

The females sat quietly for a moment.

"What is your biggest challenge right now?" Urilla Wuti asked.

"Nimida and Nootau. They spend too much time together. They know the High Council chose them to be paired with each other. If I do not intervene, every day I wait, the potential consequences become worse."

"You need to tell them they are brother and sister." It was a statement, not a question.

"I have to. They deserve to know. But Nootau has always thought that Acaraho was his father. He will not understand why we could keep him and not her. And neither will she. In this case, I am afraid the truth will do more harm than good."

"What you are planning on telling them is not the truth."

Adia lowered her eyes. "No, I guess it is not. If you are saying I have to tell them who their real father is, then I am back to destroying the community."

"Every truth does not have to be shouted to everyone from the highest point. There is such a thing as privacy. But at least those directly affected by it have a right to know," Urilla Wuti said.

"I am so glad you are here, but I need time to think about all this," Adia said.

"Of course. I will find you later. Will you take me to Nadiwani, though?"

"Certainly; but we have not even talked about the Sarnonn, Haan, and the Connection I made with him—the Connection you helped me to close—and what I learned about who he is. There is so much to tell you."

"Yes, I am sure there is. And we must make time to talk about all of that, but first I need to visit Nadiwani, and I need to see Khon'Tor's new mate with my own eyes," said Urilla Wuti, concern etched on her face.

Nadiwani was finally sitting up in bed, still regaining her strength. Her eyes opened wide when Urilla Wuti stepped in.

"Urilla Wuti! Oh, I cannot believe you are here. It is so good to see you."

The older Healer sat down next to Nadiwani and hugged her, and kissed her on the cheek.

"After all this time," said the Helper, "And what a time for you to come, when we are all sick. I do not know why you are here, but I wish you had come another time. I do not want you to become ill."

Nadiwani looked into Urilla Wuti's eyes as if checking for fatigue, or any other sign of ill health.

"I will be fine. And who is this young female?" She asked it with a smile, nodding at Tehya.

Tehya took notice, then scampered over and threw her arms around Urilla Wuti. "Oh, Urilla Wuti! I am so glad to see you!"

Adia realized she had forgotten Tehya was from Urilla Wuti's community.

"How are my parents? What has happened since I came here? And how do you know Nadiwani?"

"Your parents are fine. Happy for you, but missing you, of course. As for how I know Nadiwani, I was sent here a long time ago to help her and Adia. Now seemed like a good time for a visit.

"So, how are you doing, Tehya? How are things between you and Khon'Tor?" Urilla Wuti watched Tehya's face carefully as the young female answered.

"I could not be happier. Khon'Tor is wonderful. I was a little afraid of him at first; he is a Legend, after all. And he is so big. But he has been very kind to me, very gentle. He truly cares for me. And I love him—I do. I cannot imagine being parted from him."

Urilla Wuti neither saw nor sensed deception on Tehya's part, and was relieved. *Second chance.*

Suddenly, Tehya looked up, then she flew off the sleeping mat, and leaped into Khon'Tor's arms without giving him time to clear the doorway. He caught her easily, burying his face in her soft hair, and then gently put her down.

"I have missed you!" She beamed at the unexpected visit.

"I am pleased that you are feeling so much better." He nodded in Urilla Wuti's direction and added, "You have a visitor?"

"It is Urilla Wuti from my home. You probably remember her. She said that she was here a long time ago to help Adia and Nadiwani."

Khon'Tor nodded to both Urilla Wuti and Nadiwani. "Welcome back. Let me know if there is anything you need. I will make sure it is taken care of."

Acaraho entered the room, and Khon'Tor turned to him, asking under his breath, "Did you know she was coming? I cannot seem to keep up."

"I did not. And I know that feeling very well, Khon'Tor," Acaraho answered.

"Does anyone know how Hakani and her offspring are doing?" Khon'Tor was no longer whispering.

Urilla Wuti looked at Tehya, eyebrows raised. "Hakani? But I thought—"

"Everyone thought she died, but she did not. But I am Khon'Tor's mate. Hakani is paired to a Sarnonn. She just had his offspring." Tehya explained.

Yes, the Sarnonn; so that is how he got here. Adia and I have a lot of work to do before this is all over, Urilla Wuti told herself.

"A male Sarnonn and one of our females mated? How was the offspring born?" she asked.

"Adia gave her something to make her come early. But then that created other concerns. I will let her tell you about it," said Acaraho. "If you are looking for Adia, I think she went to check on Hakani," he added.

"Please tell her to find me when she is free," and Khon'Tor smiled at Tehya before he left.

Adia had to brace herself for her next visit with Hakani. *I am a Healer; I have to be objective. What happened was a long time ago. Stay focused.*

Hakani was nursing her offspring when Adia walked into Nadiwani's quarters.

Ithua was gathering up coverings. "Good morning, Adia. I was about to take these to wash them out. I will be back later."

"How are you doing, Hakani? It looks as if she has gotten the hang of that," said Adia, nodding toward the offspring.

"She is doing well. Have you seen Akar'Tor?"

"No, I have not, but I have not looked for him either. I am sure he is around. If I see him, I will ask him to come to you. Where is Haan?"

"He went to look for Akar."

Adia nodded, anxious for the stilted conversation to end. "If she continues to do well, you can go home soon," Adia watched for a response.

"I am sure you are anxious to be rid of me," Hakani said, not looking up.

"I did not mean it like that."

"I understand, Adia. The last time you saw me, I was planning on killing your son. It is too much to expect someone to forget."

Khon'Tor changed. Has she changed too? I wish I could believe it. "It was a long time ago. Are you alright alone here a while? Ithua will be back shortly. If you are done with your offspring, I can put her in the nest if you need to sleep."

"Thank you, but I enjoy holding her."

Adia looked at the little female. She had a darker, thicker covering than the People, definitely a Sarnonn feature. Her hands looked more delicate, not as thick and heavily padded as the Sarnonn's. Despite being born prematurely, she was as large as one of the People's full-term offspring, and her size confirmed the need to induce her.

So much for the Sarnonn and the People mating; you would have to pair a female Sarnonn with one of our males. I am not sure anyone would be willing, though. They are impressive but unattractive, Adia thought.

"So, Khon'Tor took a mate after you all thought I had died. When was that, and who is she?" Hakani was still not looking at Adia.

The Healer shifted her position, "He only did so recently, Hakani. She is very nice; everyone loves her."

Hakani raised her eyebrows, "How nice for her. I never enjoyed the support of the People."

There it is; she still harbors resentment. They need to leave as soon as possible. And Khon'Tor and Acaraho are

right. We must keep her away from Tehya at all costs.
Adia turned at the sound of Sarnonn speech.

Haan had returned without his son.

"I could not find Akar," he told Hakani.

"I am worried about him, Haan."

"Mate, we need to leave. There is too much history here for you. We need to go back to our own lives. And the others are waiting for us," he said.

Adia stepped around to where they could both see her and signed, "I am going to leave you to talk. Hakani, you should try getting up and walking around as soon as you can."

They both waited for her to leave before continuing.

Haan stepped closer to Hakani. "What has happened here is not good for any of us. They now know we have a community not far from theirs. And if Akar'Tor had not stopped me, I would have killed their Leader, and others. Not a good start to a relationship between our tribes. I will have to find Khon'Tor and talk to him Leader-to-Leader."

"I wish you had killed them all," Hakani said.

Haan shook his head. "*That* is why we need to leave. Whatever happened here still smolders inside you. I only agreed to come because Akar'Tor was not getting better, and you were with offling. And you were right, the Healer and the others helped. But it is done now.

"Plan on leaving in a few days. That will give me time to try to repair things with Khon'Tor. Nothing good can come from our staying here any longer; any other help I needed from them will have to wait."

Hakani clenched her teeth. *So Khon'Tor dared to take a new mate. I wonder if she knows yet what a Monster he is. It may be that tiny female whom he ordered the guards to whisk away when we arrived. Perhaps I should pay her a visit before we go. Haan is right; it is not over between us. But why should it be, after what Khon'Tor did to me? All those years ago he was supposed to be disgraced. He should not still be in charge.*

To Haan, she said, "All right, but I need a few days. I am tired and not ready for the long trip back, and we still have to find Akar."

Haan nodded, "A few days, but no more."

A few days are all I need, she thought to herself.

Akule glanced at the figure approaching. *He is out early.* The watcher raised his arm in greeting, but none was returned. The figure continued trudging up the path to the Great Entrance.

"Good morning, Adoeete," Akule called out.

Akar'Tor looked up at the figure speaking to him, not understanding what he had said.

When they were closer, Akule realized it was not Khon'Tor.

Akar'Tor nodded in passing and continued on his way to find Hakani and Haan.

Upon seeing Akar'Tor approach, Haan demanded, "Where have you been?"

"I went for a walk," he answered.

"That was more than a walk, Akar'Tor. You have been gone for a while."

"I needed to think, clear my head. Father, I am sorry for what I did, but I could not let you kill them," said Akar'Tor.

"You were right. We need to be on peaceful terms with these people. Killing their Leaders would not have been a good start," Haan replied.

"I did not mean to say he was my father. You are my father. You are the one who raised me and taught me everything I know."

"There is too much history here, son. We need to leave soon. What we came for has been accomplished," Haan replied.

Akar'Tor nodded. *I do not belong here. But where do I belong? The son of two Leaders and no place for me anywhere.*

"Haan, please take the offling. I should try to walk around; the Medicine Woman will be back shortly, I am sure. You and Akar'Tor can talk. Akar, come and look at your sister," Hakani raised the offspring up for him to see.

The young male squinted at her. "She does not look like any of us." *Too bad for you. You are not going to fit in anywhere either,* Akar'Tor thought.

Haan took the offspring from his mate.

Hakani rose, and after getting her bearings, she padded out and down the corridor to the connecting tunnels of Kthama. Despite the painful memories, it still felt like home with its cool stone walls, the familiar humidity rising up through the levels from the Mother Stream, the moisture dripping from the stalactites on the high ceilings. She had heard the stories that the Sarnonn once lived here, ages ago. *So they were the Ancients who built this place? That would explain the size of everything.*

She came to a familiar junction and hesitated. Haan's warnings echoed in her mind; they were leaving. This might be her only chance.

Hakani made her decision and turned down the corridor.

Kajika saw a figure approaching down the passage that ultimately led to the Leader's Quarters—a figure familiar from the distant past. He knew she had returned, alive, and paired with a Sarnonn at that. Kajika held up his hand, spear in the other, as she approached.

"You can go no further," he said plainly, stepping out to block her path.

"Do you not recognize me, Kajika?" she asked, looking at the spear in his hand.

"Yes, I do. But I cannot allow you to go past this point," he replied.

"I just wanted to see my old quarters."

"I am under strict orders. You must turn back," he said. He lowered the spear and held it across the front of her as a barrier.

I do not want to make a scene. I will have to find another way to meet this new mate.

"All right," and she turned around.

Once out of sight, she stopped to think before returning to Haan and Akar'Tor. *I am not leaving until I tell her the truth about him.*

"That was quick. Where did you go?" Haan asked.

"I went to see my old quarters, but the guard would not let me by," she answered, knowing it was going to make him angry but that he would no doubt hear about it anyway.

Haan scowled.

"What are you doing, Hakani? How could you think that was wise?"

"I need to see her. Find her. Talk to her. Tell her what a monster she is paired with!"

"Find who?"

"Khon'Tor's mate. The one who replaced me. She needs to know if she does not already. He should not still be the Leader; he is dangerous, and he must be brought down."

"You are going to cause trouble between our people. Let it go," Haan admonished her.

"But he raped me! And Adia! He forced us to mate with him against our wills. And who knows how many others there might be? But he is still Leader; he got away with all of it. He needs to be punished, not parading around with his new young mate! Does she even know what she has gotten herself into? *Someone needs to tell her!*"

Haan remembered Akar'Tor, who was standing wide-eyed with his mouth open.

"Leave. This is not for you to hear; this is between your mother and me."

Akar'Tor felt behind him for the wall and followed it around and out to the corridor.

Once he was out of view, Haan turned back to Hakani.

"Hakani, I do not know what is true anymore. You told me Khon'Tor pushed you off the edge of the path into the water. You did not tell me that you stepped off yourself. And you did not tell me you had Adia's offling with you. You intended to kill yourself and her son; Khon' Tor had nothing to do with you going over the edge."

"*Who told you that?* That is a lie. He pushed me!" Hakani flailed her arms as she paced around the room.

"It does not matter how I know. But I know it is

the truth. There is nothing good for us here, only pain and strife. We need to leave here, *all of us.*" And Haan brought his fist down on the table, nearly breaking it in two.

Akar'Tor stumbled down the hallway. *Khon'Tor forced himself on my mother? That is how I came to be? But she said he did it to the Healer too. And I kept Father from killing Khon'Tor. I should have let him do it. But I stopped him for the Healer. Maybe she will tell me what happened.*

He found Adia in the eating area sitting with an older female. "Healer, may I talk to you?" he signed.

"Of course, Akar'Tor. Do you want to talk to me alone?" she added, looking over at Urilla Wuti.

"Yes, please," he signed back. Adia noticed that she could interpret Akar'Tor's Handspeak fluently now, just as she could with Haan after Connecting with him. Whatever was causing it, it made communicating much easier.

Urilla Wuti said, "Thank you for telling me the rest. I will find you later. I am going to go to my quarters to lie down."

Akar'Tor barely gave her enough time to get up before he slid into her place, turning to face Adia.

"What is wrong, Akar'Tor? You look troubled."

"I want to know what happened between you and my mother," he said.

Adia shook her head. "Akar'Tor, that was a long time ago. It is best to leave it in the past. If you have questions, you should take them to your mother, not me. I am sorry."

Akar'Tor frowned and looked down. "Since Khon'Tor is my father, what does that make me?" he asked.

"I do not understand your question, Akar'Tor."

"Haan is a Sarnonn Leader, of the Sassen. I am Haan's son because he raised me. He is the only father I have known," he said.

"Sassen?" she asked.

"Sassen, our people. Like you are the Akassa." Adia memorized the two terms. *So, they call themselves the Sassen and us the Akassa.*

"I am sorry for interrupting you, Akar'Tor, please go on."

"So, I am Haan's son, but I am also Khon'Tor's son by blood. Do I have a place here?" he asked, looking around the room as he spoke.

Adia recognized the struggle; it was the same one she had seen in Oh'Dar. Her heart went out to him. She remembered what Acaraho had said, that perhaps Akar'Tor would be the key to their future relationships with Haan's people.

"Akar'Tor, if you had been raised here as Khon'-Tor's son, you would have the right to inherit his leadership. But you were not, so you are not in any position to step in and lead our people. You do not know anything about our culture. But as Haan's son, you do understand their culture. Is there not a place for you there?" she asked.

"I do not know what you mean," he said.

"With our people, leadership is handed down through the Leader's bloodline. Father to son. Is it not that way with your people?" she asked.

"Yes, if that male is strong enough," he said, frowning.

"So when Haan steps down, who will take his place?"

"It will not be me, and since he has no real son, it will be whoever is strongest. Whoever everyone will follow," he explained.

Adia thought to herself, *I wish, again, that our High Council would reconsider how our leadership is passed down. I am not sure bloodline is all there is to it, nor that it should be. As things stand now, Khon'Tor does not have an heir. There is Nootau, whom he cannot claim. And Akar'Tor now, who has no understanding of our ways. Even if Tehya is seeded again right away, even if it is a male, it will still be years before he could replace Khon'Tor.*

"Healer?" Akar'Tor brought her out of her musings.

"I am sorry; what?"

"I want to thank you for taking care of me. It seemed like every time I woke up, you were there. Mama is not—she was never gentle with me the way you are. I appreciate how kind you were to me."

Akar'Tor met Adia's eyes and smiled. "I am going

to get something to eat before I go back," and he got up from the bench. "My father wants to leave soon. I do not know if I want to go," he added.

"I am sorry, Akar'Tor. I know this must be confusing for you. My own son, Oh'Dar, he is Waschini. I raised him from a very young offspring. He has the same struggles with fitting in. Maybe it would help you to speak with him," she added, before he walked away.

While waiting for his food, Akar'Tor did some thinking. *Adia is so nice. How could Khon'Tor do that to her? And to my mother too. Mother is right; he needs to be punished, not revered. I do not care what Father says; maybe this is my place. Maybe I am supposed to make him suffer, for both of them.*

Khon'Tor and Acaraho were in the Great Chamber discussing plans for the upcoming High Council meeting when Kajika found them.

"Adoeete, I came as soon as I was relieved. I thought you should know; I intercepted your mate trying to go into your quarters," he said.

"My mate? Of course, she would; she lives there. What are you talking about?" Khon'Tor snapped, frowning.

"My apologies. Hakani, your first mate was trying to—"

Khon'Tor lurched to his feet. *"When?"* he demanded.

"Some time ago. I had no way to let you know without leaving my post, and I knew better than to do that."

"Where is Tehya?"

Acaraho answered, "She is still in the Healer's Quarters with Nadiwani; I am certain of it."

"Acaraho, go. Make sure Tehya is where you say she is. Make sure she is nowhere around Hakani, Haan, or any of them. Kajika, come with me. You can go off duty earlier tomorrow, but now I need you with me," and Khon'Tor stormed toward where Hakani and her family were staying.

Khon'Tor burst into the room without warning. He went directly over to Hakani before realizing that Haan was standing near the other side of the room. He turned to address the Sarnonn first.

"Haan, I do not want trouble with you. But I am the Leader here. You are my guests." His signs slashed through the air. "These are my people," he added, pounding his own chest. Then under his breath, he said, "And I will not be bullied by the fact that you can kill me, any of us, anytime you wish. I am the Alpha here!" Khon'Tor glared at Haan.

Haan nodded, raised both his palms for a moment, then lowered them and stepped back.

Khon'Tor turned to Hakani. "This guard tells me you tried to enter my quarters? I want to know *why*?"

"I just wanted to go there for sentimental reasons," she said, looking over at Haan, who was standing to the side of the room.

"Sentimental reasons? Our relationship was never comprised of sentiment. There are no sentimental reasons that you could possibly have to go there. I can *guess* why you went there. But it does not matter. Let me make this very clear. You do not go anywhere near my quarters again. You are not to go near my mate, Tehya, either. We took you in. We have taken care of you and your son. We have shown you hospitality and forbearance. And in return, you paid us with lies and by bringing infection to us all. Well, our hospitality is over. You must return to your own life and let us get on with ours."

He glared at Hakani, then turned and looked at Haan. Khon'Tor had intentionally exposed his back to the Sarnonn as a show of gall, knowing that Haan could have killed him, regardless.

Khon'Tor nodded to Haan and started to leave, Kajika behind him.

Haan followed them. "Khon'Tor," he said.

The Leader turned.

Then Haan signed, "There is no trouble between you and me. We must have peace between our people. My mate is wrong, and she no longer has any place here. We will leave as soon as I believe that Hakani is strong enough."

Khon'Tor signed, "I agree. Thank you."

He dismissed Kajika and went to find Tehya.

Acaraho and Adia were both with Tehya. Khon'Tor entered the Healer's Quarters and breathed a sigh of relief at seeing them all together.

"What is wrong?" Tehya asked.

Khon'Tor took another breath to relieve more of the tension.

"You must promise me again, Tehya. Say it. You will stay away from all of them—the Sarnonn, the female, Hakani, all of them. You have a trusting nature, so I need to hear it again."

Tehya nodded.

"Say it," he repeated.

"I understand. I will stay away from them—all of them. I promise."

"Do not misunderstand me, Tehya. There is no leeway here. They will be leaving in a few days. Then things can get back to normal. Well, as normal as possible. But until then, if they even come near you —" Khon'Tor squeezed his brows together, fists clenched.

Acaraho spoke up, "I have already set an armed guard, this time directly outside your quarters, Khon'Tor. Kajika—he is the one who stopped Hakani earlier," he added.

"I saw him when I came down the corridor. Just the one?" he asked.

"There are others spaced along the route to your quarters. No one can get to her, Khon'Tor. Hakani already tried, and I doubt she will try again. But if you prefer I can set another—"

Khon'Tor calmed himself down. *Acaraho is right. Hakani will not try that again; I am overreacting. And we are already short-staffed as far as guards are concerned.*

"No. It will be fine. But until they leave, either I will be with Tehya here, or she will be with me, and if I have to leave her in the Leader's quarters there is a guard outside. I will not trust her being alone again. Adia, is there any reason why they cannot leave now?"

"Nothing would make me happier, Khon'Tor, but Hakani does need to get her strength up. Haan could probably carry her, but I do not think she would agree to that, and we do not know how far the journey is. I am also not sure she wants to leave," Adia answered.

"The sooner this is behind us, the better." He paused. "How many more are sick? Do we know?" he asked.

"Oh'Dar said that he thinks it has pretty much run its course. But we are not through it yet. Do you still want to send Nadiwani to the Brothers?" she asked.

"It depends; how are Ithua, Honovi, and Acise holding up?" Khon'Tor asked.

"They could use a break. Nadiwani, are you up to going to the Brothers?" Adia asked Nadiwani directly.

"I would be glad to, as long as it does not shock them having one of us around," answered Nadiwani.

"It is a chance to reinforce our relationship with them. They have sacrificed a great deal giving up both their Healers to help us," said Khon'Tor.

"I will go in person to ask permission first," said Acaraho.

Khon'Tor nodded. "Adia. I need to talk to Haan again, and you seem to be able to communicate with him better than any of us. Would you help us make sure that we understand each other?"

Adia nodded.

"Right, let us go. I want them out of here as soon as possible," and Khon'Tor left with Adia to find Haan.

Haan was still with Hakani, and Adia signed to him, "May we speak with you in private?" Haan nodded, stepped out into the corridor, and followed as they led him to a nearby meeting room.

Adia interpreted for both of them.

"Haan, my hope is for peace between our people, as you said. Not because you have the advantage in size and strength, but because that is our way. We live in harmony with the Great Spirit and all creatures here—if possible," Khon'Tor spoke frankly, watching Haan's face closely for signs of understanding.

"You have nothing to worry about, Khon'Tor. I do not hold your earlier outburst against you. As I hope you do not hold my protection of Hakani against me. She is my mate, and you were on the offense. It is my place to protect her no matter what her failings."

Haan sighed and looked up, taking a moment to enjoy the fresh scent of outdoors wafting down through the room's ventilation shaft. He glanced up at the shaft and nodded before continuing, as if making a mental note.

"I have learned since then that some things I was told were not true. I have been misled about what went on between you and Hakani. Certain actions that she claimed took place, which did not, have changed my understanding of the problems between you considerably. Fortunately for me, I have had no such troubles from her."

As a bystander seeing both Leaders, Adia was struck by how candid their words with each other were, but also how clear their intentions seemed to be to find a middle ground where a fledging relationship could take root.

"I will not minimize my part in the conflict between Hakani and me," said Khon'Tor. "But there were circumstances of which I was not aware, that doomed our pairing from the start. I was difficult to deal with; perhaps I always have been. I am no longer blind to my own failings, but besides, it is all said and done. I do not wish my troubles with her to create problems between our people. I wish for you to leave with peace between us, as Leaders of our two tribes." Khon'Tor leaned forward slightly as if trying to convey the depth of his sincerity.

Haan nodded.

"May I say something? Please?" interjected Adia, partially raising her hand to get their attention.

Both nodded.

"Haan, you know that your offspring was too big to be born at full term. If you had not come here and we had not induced her, both she and Hakani would have died."

She swallowed hard before continuing, struggling to pick her words carefully. "We were lucky this time, but if she is seeded again—" And Adia looked down.

"I understand. I will—restrain myself," Haan said. "I can find another—for my needs."

"Do you need an escort back to your home?" asked Khon'Tor.

Haan shook his head. "No, several of my people came with me."

"They are stationed around here?" Khon'Tor suppressed a frown.

"They have been here all along. Despite our physical advantages, I would not enter a strange area unescorted, Khon'Tor. Any more than you would."

Khon'Tor nodded, controlling his self-repudiation. *I should have realized this. I am losing my edge at a time when I cannot afford to.*

Haan walked a few steps away and stopped as if gathering his thoughts before continuing.

Khon'Tor's stared at the male's huge, broad back, the massive lines of his muscles still showing under the long tangled mass of dark fur that covered nearly every part of him. While he waited for Haan to continue, his mind started racing.

So far, so good. Haan even accepted Adia's inquiry into very personal territory. I want an alliance with them, but do they fully know of our dark history together? Could there still be lingering resentments toward us of which we would be unaware? The High Council said they wanted us to find their population and establish good relations. I doubt the council members stopped to consider just how powerful the Sarnonn would be in person, as we did not, either. So much is unknown. There could easily be something I am missing that will come up later and bite us—hard.

Adia waited patiently. Finally, the Sarnonn turned to face them again.

"Akar'Tor is troubled. He has been for quite a while. It has been difficult for him, being different, but sometimes I worry it is more than that. He will always have a place with us, but his heart is unsettled. I wish we could stay and see if he could fit in here. But with my mate still harboring ill feelings and being unable to control her lingering animosity toward you, it is best we all leave together and let the currents of the past settle down," Haan added.

"Let me know if there is anything you need before you leave. How will we find you if we wish to initiate contact again, Haan?"

"When we leave, walk with me to the first valley. I will show you how to make a specific tree-break, which we will recognize as a sign you want to connect. We will come to you, now that we know Kthama's location."

Khon'Tor nodded. *They knew of Kthama but did not know where it was located,* he noted.

Haan took a step toward Khon'Tor, who, just in time, caught his instinctive reaction to pull back.

The Sarnonn extended his right hand, palm up. Then he reached out and took Khon'Tor's hand and brushed Khon'Tor's palm against his huge one. "That is our gesture of welcome and goodbye. It is reserved for our friends and allies," he said.

Khon'Tor turned his palm up in response, and Haan brushed his palm over Khon'Tor's, repeating the gesture. Then the Sarnonn Leader nodded and turned to rejoin his family.

Oh'Dar had finished making his cold-weather clothing several weeks before and was glad of it in the cool Kthama caves. He was feeling pressure to get back to

Shadow Ridge. He was worried about his grandmother, and he had not intended to stay this long. However, there was no good time to tell his parents he would be leaving. He looked down at Kweeuu. "What am I going to do with you? I cannot have you following me or coming after me again. You seem to be crazy about Tehya; maybe I can convince you to stay with her. I wonder what Khon'Tor would say to that?" Kweeuu wagged his tail as Oh'Dar spoke to him, but then turned his head toward the door and growled. Oh'Dar glanced up to see Khon'Tor peeking around the doorway. *That is not like him*, he thought, *to be so hesitant*, but at the next moment, he realized it was Akar'Tor.

"Hello, Akar'Tor. Come in. Do you need me?" signed Oh'Dar.

"Yes. Your mother—the Healer, Adia? She said I should talk to you." Akar'Tor walked in and looked around the room, taking in the overhead beams, the stacks of furs and hides.

"About?" Oh'Dar asked, puzzled.

"About the Waschini— That you do not belong here, just as I do not belong with the Sarnonn."

Oh'Dar remembered his mother saying that she could almost understand their language.

"What do you do here?" asked Akar'Tor.

"This is the space I work in. As you can see, I do not have the warm coat of the People. Or the Sarnonn. So I make wraps for myself, such as I have on now."

Akar came over and walked all around Oh'Dar, looking at his hide coverings.

Akar'Tor grunted, then signed, "You do female work."

Apparently, you have the same winning personality as I have heard your mother does, thought Oh'Dar to himself.

"Akar'Tor, shall we try speaking instead of using Handspeak?" he asked.

Akar'Tor nodded.

Oh'Dar continued, speaking carefully and more slowly than he otherwise would have. "My mother found me as a tiny offspring and saved me. I have lived here all my life, but a few years ago, I went to find the Waschini. I thought it would help me to find my own place."

Akar'Tor frowned but seemed to be following.

"We share the same situation; I do not fit in anywhere, either.

"Did it help you?" he asked, speaking in Sarnonn but more slowly for Oh'Dar's sake.

Oh'Dar had an idea. He started again, this time combining Handspeak with speaking out loud, using both carefully, to be understood better.

"In a way, yes. I learned that I do not fit into either world. I guess that since I look the same, I had hoped I would fit in with the Waschini. Now that I am back here, I have found that this is home. But maybe I needed to go away to discover that I will never be one of the People, but I grew up with them, and I love them. If any place feels like home, it is Kthama."

The combination of Handspeak and verbal language seemed to be working.

"Kthama—this is what you call your home here?"

"Yes. We call this place Kthama. What is your home like?" Oh'Dar asked.

"Not as big, but it is also underground. There are more people here. We used to live here," added Akar'Tor.

Oh'Dar frowned. *That does not make sense.*

"You used to live here? Who? You mean your mother, Hakani, used to live here?"

"Yes, she did," he said. "My mother did live here. But before that, a very long time ago, Haan's people used to live here," he said.

He is saying that the Sarnonn used to live here? At Kthama? I do not understand. "With the People? With Khon'Tor's people?"

"No. Before his people. We call Khon'Tor's people the Akassa, and they took over later." Akar'Tor answered, glancing absentmindedly around the room while he spoke.

He walked over to the chalked walls and the fresh air tunnel through the ceiling. "This is a good idea," he said, running a finger down the lightened wall. "This, too," and he pointed to the ventilation shaft.

"Why would the Sarnonn leave Kthama?" asked Oh'Dar, thinking, *I am starting to understand him pretty well. This makes the third language I will under-*

stand; four if you count Handspeak. I wonder if my parents know what he is telling me. It seems as if this is important.

"It was a long time back," continued Akar'Tor. "They split up. Khon'Tor's people, the Akassa, stayed here, and Haan's people left. There was no more contact, just a great divide. The Sarnonn stayed hidden, and the location of Kthama was lost," he finished.

Akar'Tor continued his inspection of the room, walking over to the corner where the stack of hides was piled, and where the grey wolf was lying.

Kweeuu put his head down and growled at Akar'-Tor, who glared back. Akar'Tor pointed at the wolf and asked, "Why do you keep a wolf? Do you intend to eat him later?"

"Eat him later? No. No, Akar'Tor. Eat the wolf? Never. We will never eat the wolf. The wolf is a friend. He is a good friend to me."

I do not think he understands me.

Oh'Dar took a few steps toward Akar'Tor, his hands slicing the air with blunt movements. He spoke as plainly as he could. "Akar, this wolf is like an offspring to us."

"That wolf is not an offspring. It is fully grown. It is big enough to feed several."

"No. The wolf belongs to me. You are never to touch the wolf. No one can touch this wolf. This wolf is *mine*."

He is not getting that Kweeuu is a pet and not a foodstuff.

"Come here and sit with me while we finish talking," and Oh'Dar took a place as far away from Kweeuu as possible.

Akar'Tor went over to sit with Oh'Dar, keeping his eyes on Kweeuu, who growled again.

"Where are the others?" asked Akar'Tor.

"What others?"

"The others. Like you. Smooth underskin, but browner. Darker. You look quite the same. They also have hair on the top only. Their eyes are dark though; like ours, not like yours," explained Akar'Tor.

He must mean the Brothers—the "Others."

"They live not far from here. They are good people," Oh'Dar replied. He was getting the hang of combining speech with the hand signs.

"You live in this large space by yourself, or do you have a mate?" Akar'Tor asked.

"No. I do not have a mate."

"Do you not want a mate?"

"I am not ready. I do not yet know where I belong. I must wait and see."

"So it helped to go and live with your Waschini? But you still do not know where you belong?"

"Yes, it helped me. I had to do it. I had to know if my original family was still out there. And I had overheard terrible, bad things about the Waschini. But I found they were not true. At least not entirely.

The Waschini I met were not bad, at least not all of them. Some, yes, it is true."

"Thank you, Oh'Dar. I am tired, so I will leave now."

Oh'Dar nodded and watched Akar'Tor rise and walk away. He turned to the grey wolf who was eyeing the door lest Akar'Tor return. "Come on, Kweeuu. We need to find my parents."

Oh'Dar found Adia in with Tehya. After greeting the others, he addressed Adia. "Mama, where is Father? I want to talk to you both," he said.

Adia's heart jumped. *He is leaving.*

"Your father is with Khon'Tor. Do we need to interrupt them?"

"It is something he might also want to hear. Shall we go and find them?"

"Sure. Tehya, please excuse us," Adia said.

Oh'Dar turned to Kweeuu and said, "Stay. Protect." Kweeuu went and lay down next to Tehya, who happily rolled over on top of him, hugging him from head to toe. Kweeuu looked up at Oh'Dar and wagged his tail.

"What was that about?" Adia asked as they walked past the guard to find Khon'Tor and Acaraho.

"Oh, I taught Kweeuu a new command. You know how I made those little cotton sheaths for Tehya? Well, I took one she had worn, and I used it to train him to her scent. He will not let anyone hurt her. Or, at least, he will do his best to stop them."

"You should tell Khon'Tor. I think he would appreciate it," she said.

Khon'Tor and Acaraho looked up when Adia poked her head into their meeting room.

"May we interrupt you, or should we come back in a while? Oh'Dar has something he wants to share."

Khon'Tor looked at Acaraho, who shrugged.

"We are done here. Come on in," and Khon'Tor waved them inside.

"What is it, son?" asked Acaraho.

"I just spent some time talking to Akar'Tor. And by the way, I can pretty much understand him now. It is not totally fluent, but if I sign and talk at the same time, and we keep it simple, it goes a lot better. Try it next time."

Acaraho and Adia looked at each other.

Another of Oh'Dar's innovations, thought Adia.

Oh'Dar summarized his conversation with Akar'-Tor, taking care not to leave out the part where the young male had said the Sarnonn used to live at Kthama.

"Is it really possible that they used to live here? If so, that would explain why everything is so big, bigger than the People need. I noticed that Haan did not have to stoop to go through any of the doorways."

"Then he asked me if we were going to eat Kweeuu, which I said definitely not. So please, keep Kweeuu away from him! Even if they are leaving in a few days, it makes me nervous," he added.

"Do not worry, son; we will look after Kweeuu. But that makes it sound like you are not going to be here to look after him yourself?" asked Acaraho, glancing at Adia. Oh'Dar looked over at his mother, then down at his feet. "Well, alright, I might as well get this over with."

Oh'Dar stood up and addressed his mother. "I am sorry, Mama. I know you want me to stay, but I never intended to stay this long, and I need to get back. I wanted to see you and return Kweeuu. But this sickness problem has kept me here longer than I intended. I hate telling you that, both of you," he looked at first one parent than the other.

Adia looked away. "It is not totally unexpected, Oh'Dar. Some of the things you said let me know you were not staying. So when are you leaving?" She choked back a sob.

Oh'Dar hurried over and hugged her. "Please do not cry, Mama. I will be back. Akar'Tor asked me if going to live with the Waschini helped me decide where I belonged. I told him it did, and it did not. I still do not fit anywhere, but I do know now that this will always be my home. This is not the last time I will see you—I am just not sure when I will be back."

Acaraho came over and rested his hand on Oh'Dar's shoulder. Oh'Dar turned, and Acaraho hugged him gently. "We are grateful you came back. I hope you will not stay away so long this time."

"When are you leaving?" repeated Adia, looking up at Oh'Dar.

"As soon as the weather breaks. I do not want to risk Storm on icy ground," he said.

Adia nodded sadly. "Let us know how we can help."

"But what about Kweeuu? What is going to keep him from going after you again? We cannot lock him up," said Acaraho.

"I have been working with him. Khon'Tor, if you would consider it, I have trained him to protect Tehya. And she likes him. He will also be company for her if you are ever away."

Khon'Tor nodded. "Be sure to let us know before you leave this time."

Oh'Dar nodded and left; all the emotions caused by his coming home were suddenly overwhelming him.

Once down the tunnel, Oh'Dar stopped to let his feelings catch up. *I cannot stand to hurt Mama. She looked crushed. Father was strong; he always is. I am glad they have each other. And I do hope I am that lucky someday, to share with someone what they have.*

Khon'Tor looked over at Adia and Acaraho and said, "You have done a fine job with him, you two. You have every reason to be proud. He has been a great help to us. When you first brought him to us all those years ago, I never imagined I would be saying that I am sorry to see him leave."

"I hoped he would take a mate from the Brothers. Acise is interested, that is for certain. And I think he is. But I wonder if his leaving will put out the fire or inflame it. It could go either way," said Adia.

Seeing that Adia was about to lose control over her emotions, Acaraho changed the subject. "Oh'Dar said that the Sarnonn lived here at Kthama long ago. It would fit the story of the Sarnonn mixing with the Brothers. Then at some point, they left, and our people took over Kthama. They may have other parts of the story that we do not have. I am not saying that it is not true. Haan and his family need to leave as soon as possible, but I wish we had time to establish more of a relationship with them."

"I do as well, to a point. And I believe in time it would be possible. But right now, I just want them gone," said Khon'Tor.

The sickness had run its course. Most everyone was back to health or close to it. Fully recovered, Nadiwani had gone to help the Brothers, and Tehya was well enough to return to the Leader's Quarters, taking Kweeuu as her companion. Hakani and Haan and their family were back in their original quarters. The People were relieved that the worst was behind them, so it was disconcerting when Khon'Tor began feeling ill just as the end of it was in sight.

Khon'Tor hid it as long as he could, spending as much time with Tehya as possible. Then, one evening as he returned to their quarters, Tehya noticed that he was taking longer than usual to complete his accustomed routine.

"What is wrong? Are you feeling alright?" she asked, as he stood slumped over at the work table.

He wandered over slowly and sat on the sleeping mat beside her, resting his head in his hands. "Just tired, that is all.

"You look beautiful by the way," he added, picking up a curl and toying with it between his fingers. He looked at her and leaned in, his lips touching hers, and gave her a look she knew so very well.

"Are you sure you are up to this?" she asked.

Khon'Tor kissed her again, harder.

Tehya responded and slid closer to him as Khon'Tor slipped an arm around her shoulders and leaned her back on the sleeping mat. Up on one elbow, he relished looking at her stretched out beside him. He let his left hand trail down the front of her, following each curve and angle. Tehya ran her fingers over his lips, and he captured them between his teeth and held them with the gentlest pressure. He moved his hand under her, down to her hips, and pulled her close. He patiently touched her in the ways he knew pleased her and waited until she was ready for him. Khon'Tor knew that once her desire built, Tehya would pull him over onto her, signaling that she was ready for him to take her. Pleasing Tehya and knowing she wanted him inflamed his own passion, but he took his time, doing everything he could to ensure her pleasure before he let himself find release.

Afterward, exhausted, Khon'Tor lay in the dark with Tehya in his arms. His thoughts felt sluggish, his head ached, and he was having a hard time collecting them. *Whatever happened to change me, I am grateful for it. Even though I admit that ordering Tehya around is arousing, I have no desire to hurt her or frighten her as I did with Hakani. Or with the others. So it is not exactly the same. The idea of Tehya being afraid of me, even a little, would break my heart. I only want to protect her and make her happy.*

His head began to pound harder. At last, he had to admit to himself that he had finally succumbed to it. *I pray that this sickness does not destroy my hopes for offspring. I pray that is not my punishment for what I did before, because it would be unfair on her. At least I was able to mate her one more time.*

Khon'Tor looked down at Tehya, sleeping next to him, her head resting on his arm. Feeling chilled, he pulled the covers up over them both as Kweeuu thumped his tail against the stone floor from his spot on her side of the mat.

By the next morning, the sickness had fully taken hold. Khon'Tor's skin was pale, and his temperature was considerably high. Tehya woke up, took one look at him, and ran to the wooden door. She pulled it open and flew outside to ask the guard to find Acaraho or Adia.

"I cannot leave my post," he said, looking down at the huge wolf that was staring up at him.

"You have to go. Please, Khon'Tor is sick. I do not want to leave him. Surely it is not that far?" she pleaded.

The guard exhaled. "I cannot. Khon'Tor was very clear that if I leave this post, I will answer to him personally."

Tehya ran back inside and grabbed a heavier wrap, Kweeuu still at her heels. "No, Kweeuu, stay," she ordered him, and started down the corridor to look for Adia or Oh'Dar.

Her feet padded along on the cold, stone floor as she rounded one corner, then another.

Where is the other guard? Somewhere I overheard that Kahrok was his name; I know he was supposed to be here, and he could help me if I could just find him—or anyone!

In her panic, no longer sure which was the way to the Healer's Quarters, she turned down the next tunnel she came across. All the corridors looked the same. Confused, she knew she must ask someone for help. She ran back down the tunnel, and even though it was extremely rude to do so, darted into the first open doorway.

"Please, can you help me? I am trying to find—" She looked up into the face of the Sarnonn.

As she was standing transfixed, there was a movement from the other side of the room as someone else came quickly toward her.

"You must be Tehya," said Hakani. She recognized her from the Great Entrance and eyed her up and down, quickly taking in the honey coloring, small stature, and fancier wrappings.

"So you are Khon'Tor's new mate," she sneered.

Tehya pulled her eyes from Haan to look at the female who was addressing her.

Haan stepped forward. Tehya stepped back involuntarily, then realized he was moving toward Hakani, not her.

Akar'Tor stood at the back, watching it all unfold.

"Hakani. Stop," Haan warned.

"I wanted to meet you. So, tell me, has he started any of his little games yet? Or is he saving them for later?" Hakani's face was now inches from Tehya's.

"What games? I do not know what you are talking about," Tehya said, frowning, and stepped back.

Haan did not understand all that Hakani was saying as she was speaking so quickly, but could see the alarm in the young female's face.

"Hakani. Stop."

Hakani grabbed Tehya's arm, pulling her forward and forcing the petite female to look at her.

"Well, he will. You will see. Khon'Tor enjoys hurting females, so he will get around to it eventually; it is just a matter of time. Remember that I told you this, the first time he takes you by force. Without Your Consent. And you can try and resist, but the more you fight him, the more he *likes* it! He may be gentle with you now but wait and see. Mark my words, it is just a matter of time. And however much you beg him not to—" Hakani kept her eyes locked on the younger female's.

"*You will stop now*. Whatever you are saying, you are scaring her," Haan repeated and stepped toward them.

Hakani laughed.

Tehya stared wide-eyed, and the color drained from her face. Hakani knew she had accomplished what she had set out to do.

The younger female jerked her arm away from Hakani. "I do not believe you. Khon'Tor loves me. He would never hurt me. He has never been anything but gentle and kind!"

She turned and ran out through the door and down the hall as fast as she could.

Haan glared at Hakani. "Why did you say those things to her?"

"I just told her the truth about what kind of Monster her mate, the great Khon'Tor, really is. *That he takes females by force and enjoys it.* How, eventually, he will get around to hurting her. It is the only way he gets his satisfaction."

"More lies? Enough. We are leaving, Hakani. Tomorrow. No more delays. I do not care if you are well enough or not; have both yourself and the offling ready at first light.

"Fine. We can leave tomorrow; I have done what I needed to do."

Hakani turned to Akar'Tor, "If there is anyone you want to say goodbye to, do it tonight."

Akar'Tor said nothing. He had been able to make out enough to have gotten the picture. Khon'Tor was not only a rapist but a sadist as well.

Tehya rounded the corner and ran smack into Oh'Dar, who grabbed her to keep her from falling.

"What's wrong, Tehya?"

"It—it—she— It is Khon'Tor. He is sick; please come!" She gasped for breath.

Within minutes, Oh'Dar had led Tehya back to the Leader's Quarters.

Khon'Tor was indeed sick—very sick.

"Keep him covered up the best you can; I am

going to get my mother and will be back as soon as I can."

Tehya could not get Hakani's words out of her mind. She sat down next to Khon'Tor, who was sound asleep.

You would not hurt me. I do not believe her. You warned me to stay away, and, oh, I did not mean to run into her; it was an accident. I cannot tell you; you will be so angry—and *after you warned me to be sure to stay away from all of them.*

Tehya lay down next to him and buried her face into the mat as she waited for Adia to arrive.

Oh'Dar and Honovi were there in no time.

"Yes, he definitely has it. Luckily we have had lots of practice. Oh'Dar, it is going to take quite a few of your pelts to keep him covered up," said Honovi.

"The Brothers may have a Bison skin," said Oh'Dar. "I can go in the morning—and I could also check on Nadiwani. In the meantime, I will go and get all the dry wolf pets I have."

"Oh'Dar, wait. If you are going in the morning, would you mind taking Acise back? We are almost done here, but now that Khon'Tor is sick, I will need to stay longer," Honovi pointed out.

Then she added, "Acise has been directly around as much of the sickness as long as I have. She has been taking the Echinacea and some other herbs I added for those of us in direct contact with anyone showing symptoms. She is also the youngest and probably the healthiest of us all. If she were going to come down with it, I believe she would have by now. And if they followed Ithua's instructions, everyone back at the village has been taking the Echinacea as well. We cannot stay holed up here forever."

"I agree with you. And I can take her with me. Even though I had the sickness, none of the others in my Waschni family came down with it. So people have different levels of resistance on their own, to begin with. Just let her know, so she is ready at first light," he said. "I will have her pony ready; she can meet me at the Great Entrance," he added. "And do not worry, Honovi. I will hold the line between us, I promise."

"Thank you, Oh'Dar."

Khon'Tor stirred and awoke to find Tehya watching him.

"Lie still; you are sick. Oh'Dar is going to bring you more covers so you can stay warm, and I am right here," she said.

"I am not that sick. I just need a little sleep, that is all," he said.

"No, not only did Oh'Dar and Honovi both say that you have caught the sickness, but it is obvious that you have. Now, please. Cooperate."

"Have you been crying?" He sat up a bit. "Please do not cry. I will do what they say. When will they be back?" he asked.

"Honovi will be back shortly. Oh'Dar is leaving in the morning to take Acise back and get some larger pelts for you."

She sniffed and wiped her eyes with the back of her hand, not directly answering his question. "Are you warm enough? Do you want me to have Kweeuu get under the covers with you?"

Khon'Tor smiled weakly. "I am sure he would do it for you; Kweeuu seems to love you, Tehya," and he looked over at the grey wolf.

Kweeuu wagged his bushy tail at hearing his name and inched closer to Khon'Tor.

"Oh, all right, come on," the Leader said, and he saw Tehya's face light up.

The grey wolf padded over and lay down next to Khon'Tor.

"Apparently, he likes us both," she smiled, grateful that Khon'Tor had granted her this pleasure.

The next morning, Oh'Dar met Acise as planned. They mounted; she on the spotted pony and Oh'Dar on Storm. The air was crisp and invigorating, but Acise was quiet, hardly making conversation, so they rode in silence.

When they arrived, Is'Taqa came rushing over to greet them. He lifted his daughter down and hugged her. "I am so glad you are home. How is your mother? And my sister?"

"They are fine, Papa. I think Momma was ready to come home, but then Khon'Tor got sick, so it will be a few days. Is everyone here alright?" she asked.

"Yes. So far, no one has become ill. Having Nadiwani here has been interesting, though. Most of our people have never been around a Sasquatch this long. I remember the day your father came in so many years ago to take you back home with all those pelts of yours, Oh'Dar. Oh, what a stir he caused then."

Oh'Dar dismounted, his feet hitting the cold ground hard, and came over to greet Is'Taqa.

"Adik'Tar, where is Nadiwani?"

"She is off with Snana, gathering some supplies. They will be back soon, no doubt."

Oh'Dar went over and pulled one of Acise's satchels off her pony. She came and took it out of his hands, the weight of it causing it to sag, "I have it, thank you."

Oh'Dar followed a few steps after her. "Acise. Please. What is wrong?"

She struggled with the bag then turned to him, tears in her eyes. "You are going back to them, yes? When were you going to tell me?"

Is'Taqa frowned, looking from Oh'Dar to his daughter.

"I was not going to leave without saying goodbye, Acise. I promise," said Oh'Dar, hurrying after her.

"Do not bother. It does not matter. You are leaving, but I know you care for me. How can you go?"

Tears were streaming down her face, and she continued to march away from him

"Acise, I am sorry. Truly I am. I do plan on coming back; I just do not know when. It is not fair to expect you to wait for me; I will not ask you to do that," he added.

Just then, Snana and Nadiwani came around the corner. In each of Nadiwani's hands were baskets overflowing with different tree barks, vines, and roots.

"What is going on?" she asked Is'Taqa.

"I have no idea. All I know is that my daughter is crying because Oh'Dar is leaving. I must have missed something important."

"Oh'Dar is leaving?" Nadiwani frowned.

"They spent a lot of time together at Kthama," she went on to explain, setting down the baskets and brushing dust off herself. "They developed feelings for each other, or figured out that they already had them; I don't know. I fear Oh'Dar is still not sure where he belongs, and so he has held himself back a bit, whereas Acise has lost her heart to him, I am afraid."

Acise dropped her satchel and ran into the family shelter. Oh'Dar joined Nadiwani and Is'Taqa. "I am sorry, Is'Taqa. I do not want to hurt her. I just do not know where I belong, and until then, I cannot commit to anyone. I will be leaving when the weather breaks."

Is'Taqa did not comment.

Oh'Dar continued, "Nadiwani, nearly everyone is over the sickness, but now Khon'Tor has come down with it."

Nadiwani chewed on her lip. *I cannot think of anything we can do that we have not already done for everyone.* "Just keep him warm, give him lots of water, let him rest."

Oh'Dar nodded his agreement and turned to Is'Taqa.

"I wanted to see if you had any Bison skins, Is'Taqa. None of the wolf pelts is large enough for Khon'Tor, though I can double them up."

"I have some you can use. Come with me."

With a little difficulty, Is'Taqa and Oh'Dar carried the Bison pelts, which they rolled and secured across Storm. As Oh'Dar mounted the stallion and was ready to leave, Is'Taqa asked, "Do you care for her Oh'Dar?"

"Yes, Is'Taqa, I do. But I do not fit in anywhere. I do not fit in the Waschini world, I am not one of the Brothers, and I am not one of the People. I cannot help but think she would be happier with one of your braves than a misfit like me. At least she could have a normal life. I am not sure what I even have to offer her.

"Please tell Acise I will stop by when I do leave. I

promise," and with that, he turned Storm and headed for Kthama.

As they rode through the valley, Storm became skittish. As before, the eerie feeling returned, and the hair stood up on the back of Oh'Dar's neck. He urged Storm on, anxious to pass through the area as quickly as possible.

Storm's hooves echoed crisply from the entrance to the Great Chamber. One of the guards came over to hold the horse while Oh'Dar dismounted. Oh'Dar dragged one of the Bison skins off and let it slide to the floor,

Having greeted the guard, he said, "I will be leaving before the next moon, and I could use your help if you do not mind. Some extra feed for Storm would be good if you can spare it, to build him up. It will be a long trip."

Oh'Dar grunted as the last Bison skin also slid onto the rock floor. It had taken both him and Is'Taqa to hoist them up onto Storm. "I am going to need help getting these back to Khon'Tor's quarters. Is there someone who could help me?"

Oh'Dar entered the Leader's Quarters, one of Acara-ho's extras following with the heavy Bison hides.

Khon'Tor was sitting up, but quiet. Tehya was in the work area, making broth as she had watched Oh'Dar do many times for her.

"Over there, please, next to Khon'Tor," he said.

The male placed the hides close, and Oh'Dar stepped forward. Together they unrolled one and tugged it up over Khon'Tor.

Too weak to protest, Khon'Tor just signed his acknowledgment.

"I am going to go to bed; I am exhausted. Will you be alright here by yourself tonight?" asked Oh'Dar.

"We should be fine. Khon'Tor will hopefully sleep. Kweeuu is here, and there is a guard outside in case I need additional help, so you can go and rest," Tehya reassured him.

Oh'Dar patted her arm before leaving. "I will check back in the morning. I also believe that Haan and the others are leaving then, if that helps," he added before he left.

As Oh'Dar started to leave, Kweeuu jumped up and came over to him. "No, Kweeuu. Stay. Protect." Kweeuu turned and took up his spot next to Tehya's side of the bed.

Oh'Dar hurried back to his workshop. He hoped that Honovi would be there. He still could not shake the feeling from the Valley. He felt exceptionally foolish, but he did not want to sleep alone tonight. He was glad to see her when he walked in.

"You are back," she said brightly.

"Yes, and Acise got home safely. I just checked on Khon'Tor; he is tired, but that is normal, and Tehya and Kweeuu are with him.

"I am finished, so I am going to turn in. You and Ithua are staying here tonight, I hope?"

"Yes, we were planning on it." Honovi stared at him, "Are you alright?"

"Yes, just tired, I guess."

"Get some rest, Oh'Dar. I am almost done here, and then I will also be going to sleep."

Khon'Tor woke the next morning to find Tehya at his side, sandwiched between him and the grey wolf who was tucked up against her.

This is the morning Haan and his family leave, he thought. *Haan wanted to show me the tree-break to initiate contact. Without it, we have no way of connecting with them again. Acaraho will have to go in my stead.*

Hopefully, now things can get back to normal. The High Council meeting will take place in a few months, and preparations must begin in earnest.

Oh'Dar entered to check on them both, sheepishly pushing open the wooden door and peering around it before entering. "Are you awake in there?" he called out.

"Come in. You must go and find your father. Haan and his family are leaving today. Carry my message to Acaraho for him to accompany them into the valley where Haan will show him a special tree-break. Tell him I cannot go."

"I will take care of it, Khon'Tor. Honovi and Ithua will be returning to the Brothers after you are well. When they do, Nadiwani will return to High Rocks. So far, Acaraho and Adia have not come down with the sickness, but I suspect Nootau has caught it."

Nootau, Akar'Tor. Perhaps this is my punishment, to be the one to break the 'Tor chain of leadership, to lose the 'Tor line forever.

Oh'Dar hesitated, "I will be leaving when the weather breaks, but until then, I am here for whatever you need me to do."

"I hope to be well long before that time, Oh'Dar."

"I am sure you will be. You are strong, and it is not life-threatening. Your tiny mate survived, and I expect you will recover far quicker than she did. I will find my father for you and then return to take care of you here."

Khon'Tor was too tired to protest.

Oh'Dar found his father and relayed the message. "This is for the offspring," and he handed his father a beautiful, soft wolf pelt.

Acaraho went to Haan's quarters to escort them out of Kthama. Remembering what Oh'Dar had said, he tried combining Handspeak with speaking aloud.

"Khon'Tor is sick and will not be able to escort you. I am here in his place. Are you ready to leave?"

Haan nodded and turned to Hakani, who was clutching her offspring, wrapped in several layers. Acaraho handed Hakani the wolf pelt, just the right size.

"My son, Oh'Dar, sent this for your offspring. It will keep her extra-warm. Take it, please."

Hakani snatched the fur out of his hands and glared at Acaraho. Haan frowned at her rude reaction and shook his head.

Acaraho stepped back and gestured toward the opening for them to go first. He then led them through the corridors and out into the cool weather. The bright sunshine promised a warmer day than usual.

Oh'Dar returned to tell Khon'Tor that he had seen the visitors leave. Adia was there by then.

"Well, that is a relief," said Oh'Dar. "Acaraho went with them as you asked. Hakani did not look very happy about leaving. Akar'Tor did not either."

"At least they are gone. Now we can focus on the High Council visit," said Adia.

"The High Council is coming?" asked Oh'Dar.

"Yes. They were here at almost this time last year, at the Ashwea Awhidi. We need to meet again on other matters."

"I will be gone well before then," Oh'Dar said, avoiding looking at his mother.

Adia waited a moment. "Oh'Dar, you have not had time to tell us everything about your experiences with the Waschini. I would like to hear more about them—before you—leave," Her voice broke.

"Do you want to hear now? Khon'Tor, are you up to listening?"

"It seems like a good use of my time; however, I cannot promise I will not fall asleep. If I do, please will someone wake me."

Khon'Tor sat up with difficulty. Adia took a seat next to them on the floor, draping her arm across Kweeuu.

"What do you want to know?"

"Anything. Any more detail you can think of that you have not already shared," his mother replied.

"What about Father? Do you want to wait for his return?"

"We have no way of knowing when he will be back. I will share what you tell us with him if need be."

Oh'Dar nodded. "It took me a long time to find them. I followed the path the Waschini riders left, and then I found the tree-breaks that I imagine my father or one of the Sentries made while following them, and they led me the rest of the journey. I picked plants and blossoms along the way that you had taught me I could safely eat. I used my dried provisions only when I had to. The first of their places I came to was a small village, for lack of a better word—what they call a 'town'. It was a collection of structures they had built, all lined up in rows.

"The Waschini live in peculiar structures—I already told you this part, Mama. Very rigid, not built at all in harmony with the Great Spirit's creation. I am still surprised that they survive harsh weather.

"A woman and her daughter came up to me and started talking. I pretended I did not understand what they were saying. For a long time, I did not let anyone know I could speak or understand Whitespeak. It was not honest, but I needed to learn about them first. Anyway, they took me in until my Waschini family could be found. I stayed there for a while. They were kind to me–even the males.

"Because of the locket you saved for me, Mama, with the little pictures in it—they found my Waschini family. Well, mostly my Grandmother. She is the mother of my birth father. She came a long way to get me. We traveled back to her home. She was very happy to learn I was alive. Again, they were all kind to me, well except two of them, who tried to kill me," said Oh'Dar, and then stopped himself abruptly.

"What?" Adia bolted upright. "You did not tell us this part before!"

"Oh, it is alright, Mama. Obviously, they did not succeed."

"And you are going *back*?" she exclaimed.

"Those two are gone; they cannot hurt me any

longer. They were the ones who had my Waschini parents killed—the scene you came across, Mama. It had something to do with my grandmother's home. The Waschini assign value to land, structures, and the things they make. It is hard to explain. Whoever killed them was supposed to kill me too. As long as I was missing, they would get all my grandmother's things when she eventually returned to the Great Spirit. Because I turned up alive, these two would have to share everything with me. That is why they had my parents killed—so they would get more. They did not want to share. Only, I was supposed to be killed as well, so when I came back it made them angry, and they tried again to kill me."

Adia shook her head.

"Anyway, those two are gone."

I also learned a lot about horses there. They pair the horses up, so the next generation is stronger, bigger, better. And then they trade them to other people who want these special horses. That is the best I can explain it. Well, you have seen Storm."

He paused, checking that Khon'Tor was still awake.

"The important thing is that the Waschini I encountered are not what the stories say they are. Some of them must be, but except for the two bad ones, all the others I met were kind to me. Welcoming. They respected my privacy—I never told them about where I was all these years, though I know it bothers them that they do not know. But I cannot.

Not unless the High Council said I should, I guess. But there does not seem to be a need to. It would just put us at risk. I think that is what you were worried about all along, Khon'Tor—that I would somehow bring disaster to our people," Oh'Dar used the same words he had overheard Khon'Tor use with Akule that day in the eating area—the words that had fueled his decision to leave.

Khon'Tor sighed. "Yes, Oh'Dar. That was my fear from the beginning when your mother brought you to Kthama. But I was wrong. You have not brought disaster. You have been a great blessing to us."

At that moment, something came together for both Oh'Dar and Khon'Tor; Khon'Tor righted a wrong by speaking the truth—the words Oh'Dar so badly needed to hear.

"You never told me why you left, Oh'Dar. But I know why. You overheard me saying that you would bring disaster to us all. You left not too long after. I have been sure all this time that my words drove you away. I just needed to know for sure."

Oh'Dar was silent. He had not admitted to himself until that moment just how much he wanted Khon'Tor's approval.

"You are my Leader, Adik'Tar Khon'Tor. What you think is important to me," he said.

Khon'Tor closed his eyes and nodded slowly.

Tehya broke the silence, "Oh'Dar, why are you going back? Why do you not stay here with us? This is where you belong."

"I need to go back, Tehya. The woman who is my grandmother, she loves me. If you could have seen her reaction that I was alive; she is all alone without me there, and I told her I would be back.

"I do not know where I belong—I am sorry, Mama, I know that hurts you. But I am not what the Sarnonn call Akassa, and I am not one of the Brothers—and I am not really Waschini either."

Khon'Tor waited a moment and then spoke, "In that case, Oh'Dar, it seems that you are not bound by having to belong anywhere. If you belong to no one place specifically, conversely, you then belong everywhere equally."

Oh'Dar blinked and tilted his head. Another moment of silence.

Adia could have kissed Khon'Tor at that moment, realizing the wisdom of those words.

Oh'Dar rose to leave. "I am going to go check on Nootau and see how he is doing. If you think of anything else you would like to know, please ask me."

As he left, Adia turned to Khon'Tor. "What you said was very insightful. I hope he takes it to heart. Until he makes peace with himself and all the pieces that make him who he is, he will find no rest anywhere here with us, with the Brothers, or with the Waschini."

Oh'Dar walked toward Nadiwani's quarters, where Nootau was resting. *Could it be that simple? Could it be as Khon'Tor said? If I do not belong to any one group, then I am also not confined to any one group. I can decide for myself where I want to be. Maybe that is freeing and not the burden I have taken it to be.*

Once outside, Haan led the way. Hakani and Akar'Tor were both silent as they walked.

I do not want to go. I want to stay here. I may not belong, but at least the People look like me, thought Akar'Tor.

Some time later, they finally stopped in a clearing that Acaraho knew well. It was ringed with Locust trees, a favorite of the People. They produced a hard wood that took a long time to decay. Haan looked around, then walked to a particular tree.

"When making the tree-break to contact us, always use a Locust tree. The height of the break, the direction of the break, the twist—all are important."

Haan looked at Acaraho, sizing up his strength and height. He reached over and grabbed a Locust, and at about Acaraho's chest height, easily snapped it backward with the break exposed. Then he twisted the broken portion.

"This break means that this is a place of meeting; it is a point along a traveled path. For you, this additional part—" and Haan pulled the twisted portion,

peeling the bark partway down the trunk, "—signi-
fies a request for contact. This is only for the Akassa."

Akassa—what Oh'Dar said they call us, remembered Acaraho. He nodded.

"Now, you do the same," and Haan pointed to a
tree next to the one he had broken.

Acaraho made the same break, though it took
more effort on his part.

"Always two together, always broken in the same
direction. Then twist and peel. It means that you
want to contact us, and we will come to you."

Acaraho nodded. *Khon'Tor will be glad to know we
can at least try to contact them now.*

He shuddered as a sudden chill ran up his spine,
and the hair on the back of his neck stood up.

A rustling from across the clearing caught Acaraho's attention. Appearing as if from nowhere was an
impenetrable wall of Sarnonn.

PLEASE READ

I am humbled by your continued interest in my writing. If you enjoyed this book, I would very much appreciate your leaving a review or at least a rating. Ratings and reviews give potential readers an idea of what to expect, and they also provide useful feedback for authors. The feedback you give me, whether positive or not so positive, helps me to work even harder to provide the content you want to read.

If you would like to be notified when the other books in this series are available, or if you would like to join the mailing list, please subscribe to my monthly newsletter at my website at
https://leighrobertsauthor.com/contact

Wrak-Ayya: The Age of Shadows is the first of three series in The Etera Chronicles.
The next book in this series is:
Book Six: Revelation

ACKNOWLEDGMENTS

I want to thank my fellow author and publishing friends who have seen me through this. Your support has meant everything to me.

85513260R00177